W9-CAW-598

WILD RESCUE

WILD RESCUE 4

TYNDALE KIDS

TYNDALE HOUSE PUBLISHERS, INC., CAROL STREAM, ILLINOIS

RED ROCK MYSTERIES

#1 BEST-SELLING AUTHORS

JERRY B. JENKINS · CHRIS FABRY

Thanks to the Tasty Kreme Donut Shoppe
for its help in the outcome of this story.
Ashley and Bryce Timberline

Visit Tyndale's exciting Web site for kids at www.tyndale.com/kids.

Wild Rescue

Designed by Jacqueline L. Nuñez
Edited by Lorie Popp

Published in association with the literary agency of Alive Communications, Inc., 7680 Goddard Street, Suite 200, Colorado Springs, CO 80920.

For manufacturing information regarding this product, please call 1-800-323-9400.

Library of Congress Cataloging-in-Publication Data

Jenkins, Jerry B.
Wild rescue / Jerry B. Jenkins ; Chris Fabry.
p. cm. — (Red Rock mysteries)
Summary: When twins Ashley and Bryce Timberline investigate the burglary of a neighbor's house, they become involved with some alpacas and a guard dog as well.
ISBN 978-1-4143-0143-3 (sc)
[1. Robbers and outlaws—Fiction. 2. Animals—Fiction. 3. Christian life—Fiction. 4. Twins—Fiction. 5. Mystery and detective stories.] I. Fabry, Chris, 1961– II. Title.
PZ7.J4138Wil 2005
[Fic]—dc22 2005000415

Printed in the United States of America

17 16 15
12 11 10 9 8

"I **HATE** it in friends
when they come
too late to **HELP.**"

EURIPIDES

"Outside of a dog a **BOOK** is
MAN'S BEST FRIEND.
Inside of a dog, it's too dark to read."

GROUCHO MARX

CHAPTER 1

❀ Ashley ❀

I wasn't trying to save anyone's life or catch thieves that lazy Sunday afternoon. I wasn't even thinking about the stuff Bryce and I would do after the last day of school. I was just trying to read a book and not doing a very good job because I kept nodding off. Do you ever do that? Try to read in bed, then drop the book and scare yourself and have to hunt for the page you were on?

I finally gave up and went to sleep. The phone woke me, and I tried to put on my best nongroggy voice. No idea why I do that either, as if there's something wrong with someone catching me asleep.

"Kathryn?" an older woman said. She sounded out of breath.

"No, she's not here right now. Can I take—?"

"Ashley, it's me. . . ."

"Mrs. Watson?"

Peanuts, her dog, barked in the background. He's a Chihuahua, so his bark sounds like someone breaking glass in your ear—shrill squared.

"Is your father home?" Mrs. Watson said.

Interesting question. Not a good one when your mind is filled with Sunday-nap cobwebs. My real dad had been dead for years. But she knew that. Sam's my stepfather.

"No, he took Mom and Dylan out to the cheapo theater to see some—"

"I just got back from my trip," she said. "Will you have him call me?"

Trip? Mrs. Watson hadn't told us about any trip. "What's up?" I said.

She tried to quiet Peanuts, but the dog was yipping his head off. "Something's wrong," she said. "Something's terribly wrong."

"You want Bryce and me to come over?" I heard the *thud, thud, thud* of his basketball behind our house.

"Would you?" She sounded like me on my first night of algebra homework.

CHAPTER 2

◎ *Bryce* ◎

I had to go top speed to keep up with Ashley on the way to Mrs. Watson's. I couldn't imagine what the problem was. She's a good friend. She lets us park our ATVs in her barn during school, and she always offers us snacks and stuff.

Fashion is not really my thing, but I couldn't help but notice Mrs. Watson's bright yellow pantsuit that made her look like the sun on its way to a picnic. She calls it her driving uniform. Ashley gave me her no-smart-remarks look.

Peanuts was barking, so I tried to pick him up, but he scampered away when we walked inside. He'd left specks of yellow on the linoleum, so I knew he was scared.

"I'm so glad you're here," Mrs. Watson said, wringing her hands. "Someone's been in the house." Then she started talking a thousand miles an hour, and all Ashley and I could do was stand there with our mouths hanging open. "I drove to my brother's in Wyoming Friday. He lives in Laramie. . . ." She told us about her brother, what they ate, what kind of house he has, how the grass looked.

I wanted to scream, *Get on with it already!*

Finally she said, "Anyway, when I got home, Peanuts sniffed and barked as soon as we got in the house. I couldn't get him to stop."

"He wasn't just happy to be home?" Ashley said. That's what I'd been thinking too.

"No, he usually comes in, I get him a bowl of food, and he curls up on his chair. The first thing I noticed was that stain on the stairs."

I knelt by the first stair, and sure enough, there was a smudge on the white carpet. Mrs. Watson is always neat and tidy, but this was hardly real evidence of a prowler. It could have been made by Peanuts—or Mrs. Watson for that matter.

I inspected the front and back doors. Neither looked like anyone had pried it open, and the windows on the first floor were all locked tight.

"Anything missing?" I said.

She looked around. "TV's still here and my video player. I haven't looked through the whole house yet."

"Did you call the police?"

She shook her head. "I thought your father would help. Besides, what would I tell them? They'd think I had a screw loose in my head."

Can't argue with that.

"Let's check the whole house," Ashley said.

I started downstairs and planned to work my way up, looking for any sign of missing stuff. I wasn't down there three minutes when I heard a scream from upstairs. Peanuts had calmed down, but now he started barking again.

I ran up and found Mrs. Watson sitting on her bed, cradling an old wooden jewelry box, Ashley standing beside her.

"My mother's brooch," Mrs. Watson whispered. "She gave it to me when I was young, just before she died." She looked up with little-girl eyes. "Why would anyone want to steal that?"

"Any way you could have misplaced it?" I said.

"I've kept it in here for years."

"Is anything else missing?" Ashley said, putting a hand on her arm.

The old woman nodded. "The diamond necklace my late husband gave me on our 25th anniversary." She put a hand to her mouth. "His ring! Oh, they've taken Carl's wedding ring!" She broke down, and Ashley tried to comfort her.

Any fingerprints on the box were gone now because Mrs. Watson had handled it.

I looked around the room and spotted a black smudge on the bedroom door. "What could have made this?"

Mrs. Watson's eyes were vacant. She just shook her head.

"Guess we have something to tell the police now," I said, reaching for the phone.

CHAPTER 3

❀ Ashley ❀

Bryce finally rounded up Peanuts and took him to the backyard. I stayed with Mrs. Watson while the police asked questions. She told them the only person who had a key to the house (other than Sam), was the paper delivery guy, Hank Krenshaw.

"Did he know you were gone?" the officer said.

"Sure. I told him not to deliver Friday or Saturday. I like to look at the ads from Sunday's paper, so it was on my front porch when I got back."

"Would you have any reason to suspect—?"

"Hank? No. I know he's a little weird, but he would never take anything. He watches my place from time to time."

"Does he live around here?"

"Up the mountain a ways. My husband knew him—he's a veteran, fought in Vietnam, I think. It can't be him."

The officer wrote on a pad of paper and walked around the house. Bryce showed him the smudges on the door and the carpet.

"No sign of forced entry," the officer said. "But we'll do our best, ma'am." He handed her a copy of the theft report. "This is for your insurance."

Mrs. Watson's eyes rimmed with tears. "I don't want money. I want my things back."

After the police left, Bryce met me in Mrs. Watson's kitchen and I filled him in.

"I know a Krenshaw," he said. "He's in band with us."

"The little guy who plays the tuba?"

Bryce nodded. "Toby." He flipped through the phone book.

CHAPTER 4

Bryce

Toby mostly kept to himself. I guess tuba players are loners.

His house sat at the base of one of the mountains in Red Rock, and Ashley and I easily navigated a route through pastures and back roads on our ATVs. The Krenshaw place was near a formation we called "Pride Rock," because it looks like the one in *The Lion King*. When Ashley wants to get me to laugh, all she has to do is grab our little brother, Dylan, under his arms, hold him high, and sing "Circle of Life."

The Krenshaw driveway was falling apart, and an old basketball hoop stood with pieces of net dangling from the dented rim. The house looked like it had been built by people late for a party. Windows weren't level, and the whole thing leaned to one side. Patches of grass grew between weeds and thistles.

Mr. Krenshaw's truck was in the driveway. A large tarp stretched across the back with blue newspaper bags sticking out.

The front door was open, and I heard the TV. I tapped on the screen door and a dog barked.

Toby told the dog to be quiet and looked surprised to see Ashley and me. "Timberline? What are you doing here?"

"Came to talk to your dad," I said.

"Hi, Toby," Ashley said.

Toby blushed. "Hi. He's sleeping. He gets up really early on Sundays. He has a regular job too, and Sunday is his day to sleep."

A train whistled in the distance. It would rumble near the Krenshaw house soon, and I wondered how anybody slept when that thing came by.

"What do you need, anyway?" Toby said.

"Nothin' really. We'll come by another time."

Mom and Sam still weren't home when we got there.

"You think Mr. Krenshaw did it?" Ashley said.

"Who else knew Mrs. Watson was away?"

She shrugged. "And it looks like it had to be somebody with a key."

"Maybe her husband gave one to somebody and never told her."

CHAPTER 5

❀ Ashley ❀

Mom and Sam rushed over to see Mrs. Watson as soon as we told them what happened. Sam gritted his teeth and mumbled something about the dirty rats who would steal from someone like her.

The next day in the band room my friend Hayley looked sad, so I asked how her weekend trip to the Mall of America in Minnesota had gone.

"Great," she said. "We had a lot of fun. But when we got back last night, a bunch of our stuff was gone."

"Your stuff?"

"Our DVD collection, lots of jewelry, my dad's new computer."

I told her about Mrs. Watson.

"No sign of a break-in there either, eh?" she said. "We have a whole-house security system. If anybody tries to get in, the alarm goes off and the police are notified automatically."

"Does anybody have a key?"

"Only our neighbor."

A thousand thoughts ran through my mind. The bell rang, and Hayley turned to hurry off.

"Wait," I said. "Do you guys get the Colorado Springs paper?"

She nodded.

"Delivered?"

"Yeah. Except this weekend. We had it stopped while we were away."

CHAPTER 6

Bryce

Everybody was excited about the band trip coming up Friday, but our final concert of the year was Tuesday night. Our band director, Mr. Scarberry, said first things first. I guess he meant we had to concentrate on the concert before we had fun, but that was hard.

I knew Ashley was nervous because she had moved up two chairs, and the girls she beat for first chair weren't happy about it. We had only a few days of school left, but these girls could make things pretty uncomfortable.

Toby lugged his tuba toward his chair. He put his mouthpiece into the instrument and got ready to sit down. Usually percussion people don't mix with the horn section, but I was curious.

"How's your dad?" I said.

"Okay, I guess. Police came by yesterday. What did you want to talk with him about?"

I shrugged. "Just a question about his route."

"You thinking about throwing papers too?"

"I don't know. Sounds pretty hard getting up that early."

"Works okay for Dad. Helped him buy a new scanner."

"Scanner?"

"Yeah, you know, you can hear police and fire station calls on it. He's got it in his truck now."

CHAPTER 7

❀ Ashley ❀

Liz and Denise plopped their books onto chairs two and three, where they hadn't been all year. I kept looking to say hello or just smile at them, but they focused on their music and their stands, obviously pretending they didn't see me.

My being number three had been fine with them. At least they had recognized that I was alive. I leaned over and waved at Hayley in chair number four. She gave me one of those wary smiles and leaned back.

Finally, Liz spoke. "So, the new first chair, and just in time for the concert. Don't you feel lucky?"

"Look, I wasn't trying to beat you guys, I just—"

"Don't you have to *request* a challenge?" Liz said to Denise.

"That's how it works," Denise said. "But I'm sure it was a flute fluke. We'll be back."

The two turned and glared at me.

I stared back. "Don't blame me. I just did my best, and Mr. Scarberry put me here."

Liz squinted at my shirt like I had pulled it off a dead raccoon. "I hope you're not wearing *that* to the concert."

Mr. Scarberry passed us with an armload of sheet music, greeting groups by instrument, as usual, in his high-pitched voice. "Morning, percussion. Morning, flutes."

Normally that amused me, but I was reeling. I wanted to be strong, to tell off the two brats, but I could barely breathe. I had to get out of here, even though the bell was about to ring. I put my flute on the stand and hurried to the bathroom to splash some water on my face—and to pray.

God, I feel like Jonah in the belly of the whale. Show me how to get out or at least how to survive. There must be something you're trying to teach me.

Mr. Scarberry gave me a look when I came back. He was reminding everyone how much the concert would count toward our final grade. Then he had us pair up for the Friday trip to Happy Canyons, an amusement park near Denver. Liz and Denise quickly chose each other as buddies. I picked Hayley. Two buses would go to the park. I hoped we could get on the one Liz and Denise *weren't* on.

A couple of the girls chose guys as buddies, and I knew they would sit together on the bus and hold hands and try to sneak away from the others. I'm all for romance, but some people try to grow up way too fast, and it's gross.

Bryce and Duncan Swift usually pair up since they're best friends, but Bryce chose Toby instead. It made me want to choose Duncan. If only I had the nerve.

CHAPTER 8

Bryce

I stopped by the art room to ask Mr. Cheplosa's advice on my investigation. He told me there were pawnshops all over Denver and Colorado Springs, even one in Red Rock.

"What's a pawnshop, and what's that got to do with house burglary?"

"Pawnshops are where people take jewelry or other valuables to trade or sell. The pawnshop owner pays as little as possible so he can make a profit by reselling these things, so people are usually pretty desperate when they sell there."

"Desperate, like thieves?"

He nodded. "Pawnshop owners aren't supposed to buy stolen items, but it happens."

He gave me the name of the one in Red Rock: Johnny's Pawn and Deli.

It sounded weird and reminded me of a place in Fairplay called Video and Feed. I wondered if people could sell their old food.

At lunch I called the place on my cell phone.

"Yeah?"

"Is this Johnny?"

"You got him."

"I was wondering if you had any jewelry—especially a wedding ring and—"

"Kid, I got a case full. You gettin' married?"

"No, but—"

He laughed. "Just come on in and I'll show you."

"But have you gotten anything in the last few days? Any old stuff?"

"I get stuff all the time. Look, I'm with a customer. Come in and you can look all you want."

I imagined Johnny making a pastrami sandwich and his greasy fingers all over Mrs. Watson's brooch. "One more thing. Mr. Krenshaw, the paper delivery guy. Does he sell you stuff?"

There was a pause. "Why?"

"Oh, I was just wondering about the scanner he got."

"Tell ya about that beauty, did he? I could get another of those if you want. Now I gotta go."

I would have bet my life that Mrs. Watson's brooch was at Johnny's. I called and told her that, but I didn't say anything about Mr. Krenshaw.

CHAPTER 9

❀ Ashley ❀

Mom knows how to listen and not say too much, like she has antennae that tell her exactly when to talk and when not to.

"How'd you feel when Liz and Denise treated you that way?" she said, sitting on my bed.

"Like I'd done something wrong. They don't care about me as long as I'm behind them, but when I do better, they hate me."

"You said you prayed?"

"Yes, that God would give them cavities in their teeth and holes in their underwear."

Mom shook her head, smiling. Of course she knew better.

Later I let slip that I had feelings for Duncan. "Mom, you can never tell anybody I said that."

"Don't worry. What do you like so much about him?"

"He's cute, he's smart, and he has nice eyes. He comes to youth group, so I guess he's a Christian." I sat forward on the bed. "What did you like about Sam? At first, I mean."

She ran a hand through her hair. "His eyes and his smile were the first things I noticed. Then he really seemed to care a lot about us. I wasn't a Christian at the time, but I think I sensed something about his heart. He's a good man, Ash. That's more than I could hope to find."

"Do you think he'll ever become a believer?"

"I pray for that every day. And for Leigh."

"Any tips with Duncan?"

She put a hand on my cheek. "Just be yourself, kiddo. If Duncan is as smart as you say, he'll notice you're different."

CHAPTER 10

Bryce

Mrs. Watson called during dinner and said she didn't find her brooch or jewelry at the pawnshop, "but they did have a tasty turkey-and-ham sub." She said Johnny told her the police had been by his store but that he never bought stolen goods. Mrs. Watson sounded as sad as I'd ever heard her, and it made me want to solve the crime even more. I had to get her things back.

Sam came in from flying someone to a convention and sat down to dinner. He pursed his lips at Ashley and me.

"What?" Ashley said.

"A guy I flew today might have a job for the two of you next week."

"Doing what?" I said.

"Do you know what an alpaca is?"

"I've seen them," Ashley said. "Like little llamas. Long necks, big eyes."

"This guy and his family are going away for a week. I told him how good you are with animals, and he said he'd like you to watch their herd. They live just behind the mountains."

Ashley looked at me like we had won the lottery. "What do we have to do?"

"Feed them and make sure they're okay. He has a dog that protects them from bears and coyotes and mountain lions."

Mom dropped her fork. "Sam!"

"They'll love it," he said.

"How much?" Ashley said.

"You can negotiate with him Saturday."

"They'll be sleeping in after the band trip," Mom said.

Sam stood and picked up a couple of plates. "Not all day."

Mom followed him to the kitchen. I sure hoped Sam won this battle.

CHAPTER 11

❀ Ashley ❀

Tuesday night we took our seats in the left side of the auditorium and listened to the sixth graders' performance. They'd come a long way in the past few months, but they still sounded like tennis shoes squeaking on a gym floor.

When we took the stage, the curtains closed. I put my music on the stand and was about to sit when someone called me from the hallway. I turned, but the doorway was empty. I went to the hall, but Liz was the only one there, and I didn't think she would be calling me.

I returned to my seat and the curtain opened. I saw Sam holding

Dylan on his lap. Mom sat beside them, clapping. Then she pointed behind me, and I turned to see Bryce waving and pointing at my music stand.

Mr. Scarberry tapped his baton, and the flutists' instruments went to their mouths. Everyone's but mine. The music in front of me was spread out to our second song. Beside me Denise fought a smile.

The auditorium fell silent, and Mr. Scarberry stared at me. I held up a hand and tried to rearrange my music. Pages floated to the floor.

Mr. Scarberry stepped toward our section. "You ready?" he said, squinting.

"I'm sorry," I said, hands shaking. "Somebody rearranged my music."

He looked at Denise and Liz. "Who would have done something like that?"

"Beats me," Liz said, and I almost believed her.

Mr. Scarberry checked my music and whispered to Liz and Denise, "See me after the concert."

Our performance stunk. I could hardly hold the flute to my lips, my hands trembled so much. After the first song, when all the parents and siblings clapped, I looked out at Mom and rolled my eyes. *See what I mean?*

Bryce caught my eye and held his chin up, as if to signal me to keep mine up too, I guess. It felt good to have someone on my side.

CHAPTER 12

Bryce

When the curtain closed I helped get the percussion instruments back to the band room. Mr. Scarberry pulled my sister and the other two aside. I heard him say, ". . . jeopardize our performance . . ." All three girls wiped tears.

Later I followed Ashley into the auditorium.

"What happened up there?" Mom said, hugging her.

Before she could answer, Liz and Denise came down the walkway, and their moms and dads met them.

"Ashley got us in trouble," Denise said. "She made it look like we messed up her music."

I wanted to tell them I'd seen them switch Ashley's pages.

Mom held Ashley close, and Dylan skipped up the aisle and hugged her legs. "I heard your fute!" he said.

Liz's and Denise's parents glared at us. "I'll have a talk with that director," one of the dads said.

"No," Liz said. "Let's just go."

Sam cleared his throat and stood with his back to the others. "How about some milk shakes at the Toot Toot Café?"

CHAPTER 13

❀ Ashley ❀

The milk shake helped, especially since the owner, Mr. Crumpus, put an extra scoop of ice cream in Bryce's and mine. Ice formed on the outside of the glass, and I scratched it away with a fingernail. I tried to keep thinking about good things, like the alpaca-sitting job, but my mind returned to Liz and Denise.

I had seen Hayley after the concert. "I'm sorry," she had said. "I didn't see them do it." I told her it wasn't her fault, but I kept thinking about the trip Friday and wishing I could stay home.

I was stunned when Mom said, "Why don't you and Bryce rent a movie tonight?"

She didn't normally let us stay up late on school nights, but she said, "You've earned it."

Bryce gave me a look like he wanted to hurry before Mom changed her mind. While Dylan finished his ice cream, which was everywhere on his face except in his mouth, Bryce and I rushed to the video store.

We were in the new movie section when Bryce said, "Uh-oh, look who's coming."

My heart dropped to my socks. Liz and Denise. It was too late to duck, and they walked right up to me.

"Happy now?" Liz said. "Glad you got us in trouble?"

Before I could say anything, Bryce stepped in front of me. "Y-you got yourselves in t-trouble. Then you l-lied to your parents about it."

"W-w-what's the matter? C-c-can't your sister talk for herself?" Denise said, smirking.

I felt my face turning red. "You guys can't stand it when anybody does better than you. You had to ruin it for me."

The man behind the counter raised his eyebrows.

Denise said, "Ashley, you're pathetic. And your brother couldn't keep time if Scarberry gave him a watch."

Liz glanced out the window and elbowed Denise as her mom and dad arrived.

Denise jabbed her finger in my chest. "Better be careful Friday. Awful things can happen at amusement parks."

After they left we went back to searching for a video. Bryce handed me an ancient one titled *Two on a Guillotine* and said we should give it to Denise and Liz.

"No matter what," I said, "I'm going Friday."

CHAPTER 14

Bryce

Later that week Mrs. Watson became sick and stayed in bed. I figured she was mostly still upset about her stolen jewelry.

By Friday, Ashley was so nervous she was imagining Liz and Denise in the barn and jumping when the phone rang.

I saw Duncan at the buses, and he asked why I had chosen to sit with Toby. Before I could think of an answer, Toby came up to us.

Duncan frowned and shook his head, walking away. "I thought we were best friends."

Toby and I sat in the very back row where we could see everything. I saw Denise and Liz get on, but they didn't see me.

It was cool and Mom wanted me to wear a jacket, but there was no way I was going to Happy Canyons with anything more than my swimsuit and a change of clothes. Jackets were for sissies.

Toby had his jacket. We sat there awkwardly for a while.

Finally I tried starting a conversation. "How do you like living—at your house?"

"I've never lived anywhere else, so I guess I like it okay."

"How do you like the tuba?"

"Fine. I like blowing those low notes that sound like gas and making the girls turn around. It's about the only time they look at me."

"Yeah, those are pretty realistic," I said.

"How long have you been playing the drums?" Toby said.

"I took lessons from a neighbor for a couple of years until I got pretty good. My drum set is in my room."

We were past Castle Rock before I worked in my first real question. "What's your dad use his scanner for?"

"He listens for bad road conditions—you know, snow and ice and stuff. Plus, he gets a kick out of hearing all the police calls."

"He buy it new?"

"Nah. At the pawnshop. He traded some baseball cards for it."

Baseball cards? "He have a big collection?"

"Huge," Toby said. "He's got copies of *Sports Illustrated* signed by a lot of the people on the covers. He uses the cards every few months to trade for something he really wants or needs. Last month he traded a baseball signed by Hank Aaron for a new set of tires."

What a waste! A valuable ball like that going for a set of Goodyears? If it was true, my case against Toby's dad was unraveling faster than kite string.

CHAPTER 15

❀ Ashley ❀

I've read that friends are your most treasured possessions, but you never really possess them. True friends will walk through hot glue just to keep you company. That's how I felt about Hayley. Even though she wasn't a Christian, she was as true a friend as I could have wanted. We've had problems, of course, but I can trust her.

Mr. Scarberry had worked it out that Liz and Denise were on the other bus, and I was glad.

When the second bus passed us I looked for Bryce and saw Liz and Denise scowling out the window. They looked like those Olympic athletes who strain for one more inch on the high jump, only these two were straining to get back at me.

"I thought Mr. Scarberry wasn't going to let them come," Hayley said.

"Somebody said their moms and dads blew a gasket and insisted. You may not want to stick with me today. If they see us, we're both toast."

"It's going to take more than those two to keep me away," Hayley said.

"Why does it feel like we're the Christians and they're the lions?"

"What do you mean?"

"Haven't you ever heard of what they did to Christians back in the days of the Coliseum?" I gave her a short course on all I knew about Rome and how the Christians had been killed by lions and set on fire as torches.

"How awful," Hayley said. "Why would they do that to people?"

"I guess they hated them because of what they believed."

"But couldn't you just say you weren't a Christian?"

"That's the thing about believing in God," I said. "You never want to turn your back on him."

Hayley remained silent.

I'd done it again. I'd found a way to end a good conversation. Maybe someday I'd figure out how to talk about important things without making people clam up.

CHAPTER 16

Bryce

By lunchtime Toby and I had ridden almost all the fun rides. We avoided the lines as much as we could, and when everything filled up, we ran to the water park.

Happy Canyons is actually two parks in one. The first canyon has roller coasters and other rides that take your breath away. The second canyon is a water park with slides and even a wave pool. We hit the water and skipped lunch so we would be really hungry for dinner.

A few hours later Toby and I were at the top of the Toilet, a ride that takes you and your inner tube up to a big tank and then flushes you to the bottom, splashing you through a tube that swirls like a real commode. Girls scream and guys try not to.

I was two kids from being flushed when I spotted Ashley at the concession stand near the haunted house. She was buying a snow cone, and I thought about yelling to her, but then I noticed something strange. In the haunted house someone in a car at the top held out a water balloon, and it looked like the person was aiming straight at Ashley and Hayley.

Most people think water balloons are harmless, but the summer before we were launching some with a bungee cord to see how far they would go. I was in the field, marking distances and protecting myself with a plastic sledding saucer. I held up the saucer to block a shot, and it hit so hard I got a bloody nose.

The hand looked ready to throw, so I yelled.

Ashley looked up and smiled, pointing. Hayley waved.

"No!" I gestured at the haunted house. "Look out!"

Just as the balloon fell, I was pushed into the Toilet, swirling down through the green tube with the force of a hundred flushes. I hit bottom and went under, wondering if my sister was okay.

CHAPTER 17

❀ Ashley ❀

I saw the water balloon just in time and backed away. It hit the concrete with a *splat.*

The man behind the stand cursed. "Where'd that come from?"

I pointed, but whoever had thrown it was gone.

"Could have hurt somebody," the man said. "Get kicked out for that."

Hayley and I ran to the haunted house, but the cars ended on the other side and I saw no one I knew.

"That had Liz and Denise written all over it," Hayley said.

Hayley and I headed to the common area. We were all supposed to meet there soon, so Mr. Scarberry and the other adults could make sure we were all okay.

"Do you want to ride the Brain Buster?" Hayley said.

"Not me," I said. "I'll just watch. Then we can go to dinner."

I spotted a gift shop and stepped inside to look for something for Dylan. He likes cars, stuffed animals, and just about anything. I found a little tiger key chain for a few dollars and kept looking around, keeping an eye on the spot where Hayley was supposed to meet me.

After about 15 minutes I got worried. What if something had happened on the ride? I went to the ticket area. No Hayley. I described her to the woman taking tickets, and she shook her head.

CHAPTER 18

◎ *Bryce* ◎

Toby and I changed in the locker room and walked back to the other park. On the way I noticed Ashley's friend Hayley talking with a girl I hadn't seen before. The girl held a huge stuffed giraffe, and Hayley looked concerned. I wondered where Ashley was, since they were supposed to be buddies, but by the time I got to her, Hayley had run the other direction into the crowd.

You learn a lot about people at an amusement park. Working with them in class is different than playing, and Toby was a lot of fun. I started feeling bad about thinking his dad had stolen Mrs. Watson's jewelry. The facts were not adding up. Plus, if he stole stuff at Hayley's house, how did he get in without tripping the alarm?

"Bryce! Over here!" someone called.

It was Ashley, waving frantically. I hurried over, looking at my watch.

"Hayley's gone," she said. "Disappeared."

"I just saw her run that way," I said.

"What? But it's time—"

"She'll meet us there," I said. "Come on."

CHAPTER 19

✾ Ashley ✾

I've never seen Mr. Scarberry so upset. I told him I would keep looking for Hayley, but he gritted his teeth and ordered me to sit down. He made the whole group stay put—"the consequences," he said, "for breaking the rules."

"This stinks!" somebody said.

One of Bryce's percussion mates scowled at me. "Why'd you have to mess it up for the rest of us?"

I racked my brain, trying to think where Hayley might be. There couldn't have been a mix-up about the meeting place. But what about Bryce seeing the girl with the stuffed giraffe? What had she said to Hayley to upset her? Could someone have kidnapped her? My knees trembled.

Duncan walked past Bryce and didn't say anything, which was unusual.

The smell of corn dogs, popcorn, cotton candy, and funnel cakes wafted over us. It should have been such a happy day, but people were glaring at me.

"Look," Toby said.

A girl walked by carrying a huge giraffe.

Bryce said, "That's her!" And we both bolted for her.

Mr. Scarberry yelled at us, but I wasn't about to stop.

The girl turned and stared like we were space aliens. She was about our age, with freckles and red hair. An oversized hockey jersey reached her knees. She took a step back, clutching her giraffe.

"You talked to my friend Hayley," I said. "What did you say to her?"

She frowned. "Are you Ashley? You don't look hurt."

"What do you mean, hurt?"

"These two girls said they'd give me this giraffe if I'd do them a favor. They pointed to this girl Hayley on the Brain Buster and said a friend of hers, Ashley, was hurt really bad. They said they had to go or they'd get in trouble and would I give Hayley the message. She was supposed to meet the ambulance in the parking lot."

Mr. Scarberry ran over, but before he could scold us, I explained.

"Let's hope she's still there," he said. He turned to Giraffe Girl. "Do you see the two girls who gave you the giraffe?"

She scanned the crowd and shook her head. Frankly, I didn't see them either.

Mr. Scarberry found a security guy to radio someone and have them look for Hayley. The parking lot was on the other side of the park.

Several minutes went by. The walkie-talkie clicked. "No response here. Sorry."

CHAPTER 20

Bryce

Soon it seemed everyone was whining about being stuck here. Some waved their soggy swimsuits.

"Come on! Let us go!"

Mr. Scarberry stood on a table and announced that Hayley was missing. "No one's going anywhere until we find her."

Some flute players gathered around Ashley, but Liz and Denise didn't join them. I found them at the back of the meeting area and was about to point them out to Giraffe Girl when an alarm sounded and the loudspeaker system came to life, paging Hayley Henderson throughout the whole complex.

Rumors spread like dust bunnies under my bed. Someone heard Hayley had been led away by a stranger. Another said a police helicopter chase was under way. A third said she had drowned in one of the water rides.

Ashley grew pale. I'd never seen her this worried.

Then another call came over a nearby security guard's radio. "We've found something."

CHAPTER 21

❀ Ashley ❀

My heart nearly burst through my rib cage. What in the world did "something" mean, and why didn't they say they'd found "her"?

Bryce put his arm around me as Mr. Scarberry and the chief of security ran off. The wait was killing me, and all I could do was pray.

Finally I saw Mr. Scarberry's grim face through the crowd and beside him, Hayley. Her eyes were red and her lips trembled.

Everybody just stared.

I ran and hugged her. "Where'd you go?"

"When that girl told me you were hurt, I forgot the rules. The ambulance didn't come, and I tried to get back in, but I was stuck outside the big fence. When they called my name over the loudspeaker I just about lost it. I knew Mr. Scarberry would be furious."

I looked at Liz and Denise. Since Giraffe Girl had left, they had come out of hiding. "They're so mean," I said.

Everybody whooped when Mr. Scarberry announced that we would stick with our schedule and stay until 9 p.m.

Duncan held out a stuffed unicorn with pink rings around its horn and wearing purple shoes. "Hayley, would you like this?"

"I'd love it," she said.

Duncan smiled and walked off.

I took a deep breath and let it out. I was actually jealous of Hayley, in spite of what she'd been through. It would have almost been worth it to get a gift—or even the time of day—from Duncan.

Skeeter Messler brought me a green ring with a spider on top. "I won it for you," he said.

I wondered how much money he'd dropped down the skee-ball slot for that worthless piece of plastic. "Thanks."

Mr. Scarberry turned to Hayley and me. "You two stick with me the rest of the evening."

"If it's okay with you, I'd like to just wait on the bus," I said.

"Me too," Hayley said.

CHAPTER 22

☺ *Bryce* ☺

Toby and I went down the Toilet again and were still drenched at the end of the night. There was no way a kid this much fun could have a thief for a father.

Sam picked us up and just shook his head when he heard the story. He handed me a police report from the local paper. I read:

> A Red Rock woman returned from a short vacation to find several valuable items missing from her jewelry box. There were no signs of forced entry, and the woman said no one else has a key to her house.

"Same MO as with Mrs. Watson," Sam said.

"MO?"

"*Modus operandi.* Latin for 'mode of operation.' It means how they do it."

"Does this mean we can't go on a vacation this summer?" Ashley said.

"No, it means you two have to figure out who's doing this before we go."

CHAPTER 23

Ashley

I was so tired I couldn't hold my eyes open. But as soon as I got in bed I started thinking about Liz and Denise, and my eyes popped like gourmet Orville Redenbacher's. I lit my candle and tried to write in my diary, but all I could write was *I hate them!* over and over.

I looked for a verse that would help, but I have to admit I was hoping for something like, "If people mistreat you, put poison ivy in their backpacks" or "If someone causes you heartache and trouble, make them pay."

What I did find was a place in Matthew where Jesus says:

"You have heard the law that says, 'Love your neighbor and hate your enemy.' But I say, love your enemies! Pray for those who persecute you! In that way, you will be acting as true children of your Father in heaven."

So was I supposed to hug Liz and Denise and tell them I loved them? They'd probably just step aside and let me fall and break my nose.

Jesus said, "If you love only those who love you, what reward is there for that? . . . If you are kind only to your friends, how are you different from anyone else?"

God, you can't expect me to love Liz and Denise, can you? It's too hard.

I waited for some kind of answer—you know, thunder or lightning or even a car honking. But nothing came.

The more I thought about the trip, the more I realized I was not just ticked at Liz and Denise but at Hayley too—not to mention Duncan. He had given *her* the stuffed animal, and I was stuck with the creepy spider ring from a guy who's called Skeeter because he looks like one.

"If you are kind only to your friends, how are you different from anyone else?"

I prayed, *They don't even think they're doing anything wrong. How can I forgive people like that?*

No thunder. No lightning.

On my nightstand was a picture of my father, who'd been killed years ago in a plane crash caused by terrorists. Did I have to do good to terrorists too?

I closed my diary and my Bible and blew out my candle. "I can't forgive those two," I whispered. "I don't know how. And I don't want to know how. They don't deserve to be forgiven."

Do you?

It wasn't an actual voice. It was just a question in my head.

I was hoping it was the funnel cake I had before getting on the bus (I've heard food can make you dream weird things), but maybe it was my conscience.

No, I don't deserve to be forgiven, I prayed, *but at least I asked. If Liz and Denise never ask, it's not the same thing. Is it?*

Nothing.

No thunder.

No lightning.

Just sleep.

CHAPTER 24

Bryce

Sam took us to the alpaca farm the next day. Ashley seemed really exhausted, and I figured it was because of her medicine. She has to take pills every day to keep her from having seizures, and they make her tired.

The alpaca owner, Mr. Morris, is from Arkansas and has a long, drawn-out way of talking. He met us at the front gate and punched the code, then led us to the barn. It had a red roof and lots of fence wire running around two big pens.

First we met Buck, a huge white dog that sniffed at our legs. I guess he smelled our dogs, Pippin and Frodo.

"Can we pet him?" Ashley said.

"Sure," Mr. Morris said. "He's a little cautious about strangers, but he'll warm up to you."

"What kind of dog is he?"

"A Great Pyrenees," Mr. Morris said. "They're especially good with alpacas."

"Do they herd them?" I said. "You know, like those dogs that herd sheep."

"No, they're more protectors. They'll fight a bear or a coyote or even a mountain lion that's after one of the babies. Buck here has a couple of scrapes from some domestic dogs that tried to get in the pen." He pulled Buck's hair back and showed us wounds on his legs. "Those dogs will think twice 'fore they come around here again."

CHAPTER 25

❀ Ashley ❀

I would have agreed to work at Mr. Morris's farm if only for the chance to meet Buck. He's a beautiful dog, and after sniffing us, he was friendly and let me pet him.

Holding the baby alpaca almost took my mind off Liz and Denise. It was so cute and the softest thing I've ever felt in my life. No wonder people love sweaters and hats made from their fur.

The baby is called a cria (you say it CREE-uh), and female alpacas usually have one per year. The pregnancy lasts 11½ months, and then the female gets pregnant again right away.

"How long do they live?" Bryce said.

"As long as 20 years," Mr. Morris said.

He said alpacas come in about 20 natural shades, from pure black to white and everything in between. Mr. Morris's herd of about 40 looked like a rainbow.

The baby's name was Milk Dud—because he was born yellow and brown, like the Milk Duds box. All the time I was holding him, his mother followed me around with that long neck, eyeing me with her big eyes.

It didn't surprise me when Mr. Morris told us alpacas are from the camel family, because they look a little like them. But they're closer to llamas.

When we walked into the barn, I noticed a funny sound, like humming.

Mr. Morris said alpacas do that when they're unsure of something. "They communicate with sounds and body language. It's really amazing."

They all came over and gathered around, like they were inspecting us. I've been around cows before, and they pretty much just want to eat and poop and ignore you. But these animals seemed really smart, curious about us.

Mr. Morris told us an ounce of alpaca fur is worth more than my weekly allowance, and they produce 6 to 10 pounds of fleece each year.

"We're shearing them just before we leave, so they'll look a little different. It's their summer buzz cut."

A big one stood off by itself out in the field.

Mr. Morris said, "That's Samson, one of our males. We keep them separated from the females until it's time for them to breed." He pointed to the corner of the barn. "Back there in the shadows is Whitney. She'll have her baby in a couple of weeks, probably just after we get back from vacation."

Whitney had a rich brown coat and a white face. A tuft of lighter brown fur covered her eyes and made it look like she was wearing a stylish hat.

Mr. Morris told us he used to work for a computer company in Denver that wanted to move him to California. "So I quit and bought this farm. Then I had to figure out what to do with it. Our kids are still small, and we homeschool them, so we thought about cattle or sheep, but they're too messy. Then we heard about alpacas."

He lifted one of the animal's legs and showed us its foot. It looked a little like the pad on a dog's foot. "Cows have hooves that tromp down the grass, so we'd have to have hundreds of acres to raise them. But we can raise a lot of alpacas on a few acres."

"And alpacas aren't messy?" Bryce said.

Mr. Morris shook his head. "They're like cats. They just go in one place."

"Who lives over there?" I said, pointing to a huge house near the mountain.

"The Rugers. They got a daughter about your age."

CHAPTER 26

Bryce

Ashley fell silent, and I knew why. Ruger was Denise's last name.

Mr. Morris showed us what to do. The alpacas ate in the field during the day but needed a supplement, which looked like small dog food pellets, added to their troughs in the afternoon.

I was glad we wouldn't be taking care of animals that would be on someone's dinner table the next day. The worst that would happen to these was a painless haircut.

"As for Whitney, just keep her calm. She'll want to stay in the barn. If she gets spooked or acts stressed, that can affect the pregnancy, so you'll want to call the vet." Ashley was taking notes, and

Mr. Morris handed her a card with the vet's phone number on it. She copied the number down and stuck the card in her pocket.

We were to come each morning and evening to feed and check on the animals. "Buck will look after them while you're not here, but you'll need to keep his water and food dish full too." He showed us where the dog food was kept.

"Thanks for calling," someone said inside.

I jumped. It certainly didn't sound like anyone's wife.

"That's Lewis, our parrot. My wife will tell you what to do with him. I'd like to duct tape his beak, but that's me. Come back tomorrow morning, and we'll run you through an average day."

"We'll come over on our ATVs before church. That won't scare them, will it?"

Mr. Morris chuckled. "They might look up as you drive in, but that's about it. Strange dogs or cats moving around their pens will upset them." He gave Ashley the number to punch at the front gate. "Hey, you could spend a few nights here while we're gone. We've got satellite TV and pizza in the freezer."

I thought I saw Ashley glance at Denise's house. "We'll see," she said.

CHAPTER 27

❀ Ashley ❀

Mom was still nervous about the mountain lions, bears, and coyotes, but Sam convinced her that Buck would take care of us as well as the alpacas.

The cool air felt good on my face as we rode through the field the next morning, past the red rocks that rose behind our house, and around a couple of small ponds. Summer vacation, which had seemed so far away, was almost here. Just a few more days of school.

The farm looked peaceful in the morning light, with dew glistening on the grass. I could see why Mr. Morris would move from the city to a place like this.

Up on the ridge the sun glared orange off the front windows of

Denise's house and made it look like a huge jack-o'-lantern. I had to wonder if Mr. Morris had asked her to watch the alpacas. She probably laughed in his face.

I punched the access number on the keypad, and the gate opened. Buck barked and met us halfway up the driveway. It wasn't until we took off our helmets and got off our ATVs that he smelled our clothes and calmed down.

Mr. Morris met us at the barn with his wife and three boys.

"We're going to an island!" the youngest said.

His mother drew him in. "Tell Ashley what you're going to do there."

"Fish and cook out and hi-bear-nate," he said.

"Hibernate," another boy snarled.

"Whatever."

"What island?" Bryce said.

"It's off the coast of Washington state," Mrs. Morris said. "No phones, no electricity, just the cabin, the coast, and a week of relaxing."

"Sounds like heaven," I said.

Mrs. Morris nudged her husband, as if reminding him of something. "Uh, yeah, listen, I know you're going to do fine. I do need to tell you—not to worry you or anything—that these animals are purebred, so they're pretty expensive."

"How expensive?" Bryce said.

"Well, Whitney in there is probably worth about $25,000 because she's pregnant."

My jaw fell. "That's as much as a new car. A nice new car."

"The others are worth anywhere from $10 to maybe $20,000." He nodded toward one of the males. "I'm not sure I should tell you how much Max is worth."

"Please?" Bryce said.

"One of his brothers—and he doesn't have as nice a coat as Max—sold at auction a few weeks ago for $375,000."

Bryce and I just stood there with our mouths hanging open. Finally Bryce snickered. "Proves guys are a lot more valuable than girls."

Mr. Morris said they were so valuable because there weren't that many in America. "Ours come from Bolivia. They're some of the finest in the world, so it pays to have a pure bloodline."

Mr. Morris showed us how to lead the alpacas out of the barn, clean the stalls, put fresh water in the troughs, and prepare their food. Then he showed us how to bring them back in at night, which he said they'd pretty much do themselves. Whitney stood in the corner of her stall, pacing as she watched.

"I need to go get ready for church," Mr. Morris said. "Stay as long as you like."

I wandered into the field while Bryce poked around in the barn. Samson stuck his head across the top of the fence, sniffed, and grunted. The females didn't seem to notice.

Buck loped up beside me and sat, his tongue lolling. I patted his head. He bristled and growled as a rattletrap car passed the driveway. It slowed and I tried to see inside, but I couldn't.

CHAPTER 28

Bryce

Most of the houses that had been burgled were different. Only one had an electronic alarm. Some had kids living there (who could have talked with friends about going away), but Mrs. Watson and the other elderly lady who lost jewelry hadn't.

How had anyone found out that Mrs. Watson was going away? She was such a loner. If I was going to find Mrs. Watson's jewelry, I had to figure that out—and fast.

I wrote:

Delivery people
Police

Church people
Neighbors/acquaintances
Mr. Krenshaw

I called Mrs. Watson. She sounded weak. Before I could even ask anything, she told me Mr. Krenshaw had come to her house.

"His son told him what had happened—I guess he heard from you, Bryce. I think he feels worse about the stolen items than I do. He said he'd do anything to help get them back and that he was sorry he hadn't taken better care of my place."

I circled Mr. Krenshaw's name. If he was guilty, would he do this? Was he trying to look innocent, or was he innocent?

I asked her again if she might have told anyone she was going to be gone.

"No. Like I told the police, I don't publicize my trips."

CHAPTER 29

❀ Ashley ❀

It was hard to go back to school. I kept telling myself there were only four days left and that I'd be taking care of alpacas soon. The class I dreaded most was band. The thought of it curled my stomach. I saw Hayley in the hall before class and took her hand.

"I need some help in here," I said.

"You and me both."

Liz and Denise were sitting in the first two chairs, like it was territory they had staked out a hundred years ago. Instead of making a scene, I sat in the third, next to Hayley.

There was whispering as Mr. Scarberry greeted the sections. He paused at the flutes, then continued to his desk. "You all have a good time Friday?" he called out.

People groaned.

"Aw, come on. It was better than that, wasn't it?"

"We didn't get to throw you in the pool," somebody said.

"Yeah, isn't that a tradition?" Duncan said.

"Maybe next year," Mr. Scarberry said. "Music out, please, and will the flutists please sit in their correct chairs?"

My face was hot. Did he have to do this?

"Now!"

"You're dead," Liz said, as the three of us clumsily moved.

After class, Mr. Scarberry stopped Hayley and me. "How do you two feel about Friday?"

"Like we caused everybody a lot of trouble," Hayley said, "but it really wasn't our fault."

Mr. Scarberry nodded. "You should have stayed together, but I agree. There's more going on here, and I hope to get to the bottom of it."

"What did that mean?" Hayley said as we walked into the hall.

I shrugged, then caught my breath as I saw Liz and Denise in front of my locker.

"Timberline," Denise said, sneering, "saw you at the farm yesterday."

"Yeah," I said. "So?"

"You watching the herd while the Morrises are away?"

"Why?"

"They asked me first, but I don't need a job." She leaned close. "Be careful. A bear or a coyote could snatch one of those little ones right out from under your nose. Then how would you feel?"

I clenched my fists and gritted my teeth. "Don't you dare threaten me, Denise! And don't you dare threaten those animals!"

Denise stepped back as if caught off guard, then seemed to recover. She smiled impishly. "Just be careful, that's all."

"Way to go, Ash!" Hayley whispered as they walked away. "You actually yelled."

I opened my locker and saw my WWJD sticker on the back of the door. *Would Jesus have yelled at them?*

After what he did to the money changers in the temple, I wasn't so sure. I didn't know how I was supposed to feel.

CHAPTER 30

Bryce

After school I stopped in to see Mrs. Watson. Peanuts barked his head off when I knocked and was still barking when Mrs. Watson opened the door. She was in her robe, looked pale, like she'd been inside for three weeks, and had bags under her eyes. I was used to seeing her working in her garden in a big, floppy hat, so this was weird.

"Come on in, Bryce honey," she said. "Let me get you a snack."

Mrs. Watson's snacks are legendary. At Halloween her place is everyone's favorite.

She poured me a glass of milk, then took several cookies from a Ziploc bag and put them in the microwave.

"You feeling okay?" I said.

She ran her hand lightly across the tablecloth. "Just my old bones giving out. I'll be all right."

I dipped a cookie into the milk. The chocolate was still warm and left swirls in the milk. "About last week. Are you sure you couldn't have said something to someone at the grocery store, to one of the neighborhood kids, maybe the mailman?"

"I've been over this with the police and you, Bryce."

"I know, and I'm sorry, but—"

The phone rang. When Mrs. Watson answered it in the living room, I noticed a calendar on a small desk in the corner. One day said *carpets cleaned*, and another said *pharmacy refill.* Two days before she had left on her trip a note said *oil change.* It had a check mark beside it.

I finished my last cookie and headed toward the front door.

"It's my brother," she said, covering the phone. "Talk to you later."

"Thanks for the cookies," I whispered.

CHAPTER 31

✾ Ashley ✾

When I got home Leigh was on the front porch looking through the newspaper for a used car. She didn't have any money, but it doesn't hurt to dream.

I was surprised when she said, "What's wrong with you?"

"Nothing."

"Boyfriend trouble?"

"I wish," I said.

Leigh hadn't been the most excited person in the world when Mom, Bryce, Dylan, and I moved in, and she was even less thrilled when we became Christians. So I'd kept my distance, not wanting to be the needy stepsister.

"You look like somebody just swallowed Frodo," she said. "What's up?"

"Some girls in band are jerking me around."

"Band girls. Moved ahead of them, did you?"

"Yeah."

"You want Randy to beat them up?"

I couldn't help smiling, thinking about Leigh's boyfriend squaring off against Denise and Liz with his big muscles.

"What'd they do?" she said, putting the paper down.

She cringed at the Happy Canyons part, and when I finished my story she shook her head. "Maybe you can get that dog at the alpaca farm to attack them."

"No, seriously. Any real ideas?"

She bit her lip. "I'm not into the 'turn the other cheek' thing. I'd fight fire with fire. Go after them."

I sat. "Like how?"

She shrugged. "Put alpaca poop in their backpacks. Something like that. Make their lives as miserable as they've made yours. That'll stop them."

CHAPTER 32

Bryce

Instant Oil Change is the only oil-change place in town and it's not far, so I left my ATV and walked. I put my backpack on the counter and was welcomed by a girl about Leigh's age. She wore an Instant Oil uniform with *Jan* on her shirt. A jet-black ponytail stuck out the back of the hat she had pulled low. Her eyes were really pretty and made my stomach flutter.

"Can I help you?" she said in a sweet, soft voice.

"I-I-I was wondering . . . a friend of mine, Mrs. Watson, came by here last Wednesday. Y-y-you weren't working, were you?"

"I know Mrs. Watson." She smiled a bright smile that could have been used on one of those teeth-whitening commercials. "Hang on." She stepped through the garage door and hollered, "Pete, did you help Mrs. Watson last week?"

When Jan returned she said, "Pete says we did her car the middle of last week." She tapped on her computer and studied the screen. "Yeah, Wednesday. Why? Everything okay?"

I don't know why I get so nervous around girls. My palms sweat and my throat dries up. It's the same feeling I get with pop quizzes. "I'm trying . . . to help her . . . her car . . . thing."

"Her car thing?" she said, clearly enjoying this.

"Did she happen to tell anyone she was headed out of town?"

Jan squinted. "Not me. I can check with Pete."

"Don't bother him now. Just let me know if you find out." I gave her my name and number.

"What's this about?" she said.

"Some stuff of hers was taken while she was gone," I said. "I'm trying to help her find it."

Jan's eyes grew wide, and she pushed her hat back. "No kidding? Well, you're awfully nice to help her."

I chuckled, but I was nervous and my laugh sounded weird. "I gotta go," I said, heading for the door.

When I got outside, I could finally breathe.

"Excuse me?" someone said behind me. It was Jan, carrying my backpack. "You'll probably need this."

"Yeah . . . thanks."

"Hey, you're not implying that anybody here knew Mrs. Watson was going to be gone and—"

"Oh no. I'm just looking for any clues I can find."

"Well, tell Mrs. Watson Jan said hi."

CHAPTER 33

❀ Ashley ❀

Leigh gave me some deliciously devious ideas. I went upstairs and pulled out my diary. I lit my scented candle and started in on my plan to get back at Denise and Liz. I still had three days to make their lives as miserable as they'd made mine.

1. Liz and Denise walk under a door with a bucket balanced on top.
2. Liz and Denise sit on glue in chairs in band room.

I was coming up with my third idea, something involving the lunch room, ketchup, and mayonnaise, when I thought again about the sticker in my locker. *Is this what Jesus would do?*

If my goal was to act like Jesus, I couldn't try to get revenge.

But they need to be taught a lesson.

I wrote: *Jesus never had band with Liz and Denise. And his dad never got killed by terrorists.*

I opened my Bible and looked for 20 minutes for where it says Jesus experienced every temptation we have. I finally found it in Hebrews. It was just after where it says that God's word is sharp like a knife and cuts into our inner thoughts and desires.

> *Nothing in all creation is hidden from God. Everything is naked and exposed before his eyes, and he is the one to whom we are accountable. So then, since we have a great High Priest who has entered heaven, Jesus the Son of God, let us hold firmly to what we believe. This High Priest of ours understands our weaknesses, for he faced all of the same testings we do, yet he did not sin. So let us come boldly to the throne of our gracious God. There we will receive his mercy, and we will find grace to help us when we need it most.*

Jesus must have been tempted to lash out at people who were unkind to him. He must have been frustrated that his family and even his own disciples mostly didn't understand who he really was.

I wrote:

> God, I need to understand how to act toward Liz and Denise. If you're going to use me to show them your love, you have a lot of work to do, starting with me.

CHAPTER 34

☺ *Bryce* ☺

Before school the next day I stopped at Mrs. Watson's. She's usually there to wave at Ashley and me, but I figured she was still sick. Her car wasn't in the driveway either, which was odd.

I knocked and heard something strange. Silence. Not even Peanuts barking. What if the robbers had come back? What if she was in there right now, bleeding, and I was her only hope?

Maybe the police had called and found her things. Or maybe she had gone to visit her brother again.

She never answered the door. I thought about calling the police but decided to check back during lunch.

CHAPTER 35

✾ Ashley ✾

I walked into school determined to be the best Christian ever—until, that is, I noticed a sign taped to my locker: "Ashley is a log head."

A hand reached out and tore it down. It was Skeeter Messler, and he had several other pieces of paper under his arm. The top one read: "Ashley is a spaz. Take your medicine!"

"Sorry you had to see these," Skeeter said. "Don't pay any attention to them. Just dumb people trying to have fun, I guess."

I passed Mr. Forster, our principal, as I headed to band class. He held wadded-up paper in his hands. “Ashley, do you know anything about these notes with your name on them?”

“No, sir,” I said. “I just saw a couple of them myself.”

He frowned. “I heard what happened at Happy Canyons Friday. Meet me in my office after lunch.”

CHAPTER 36

Bryce

I was relieved to see Mrs. Watson's car in her driveway at lunch. Peanuts barked and scratched on the door when I knocked. Finally, Mrs. Watson invited me in. "I was worried when you weren't here this morning," I said.

"Oh," she said weakly, looking no better than the last time I had seen her. "Had to drive to the Springs to find a pharmacy open that early. You hungry? Can I get you some lunch?"

I wished I hadn't eaten my sandwich on the way. "No, thank you." I told her about Jan saying hello and she smiled.

"I've known her since she was just a little thing. Makes a nice-looking grease monkey, don't you think?"

I nodded.

"What took you there, anyway?" she said.

I told her.

"Well, you're becoming quite the detective, but I don't know how many times I have to tell you that I didn't tell anyone I would be gone."

"Did you take your car anywhere else before the trip?"

She put a hand to her chin and looked at the ceiling. "Not that I recall. Just the grocery store and the gas station. The library."

"When you get your oil changed, do you leave the keys in the car?"

"Mm-hm. I usually sit in the waiting room, but last week I went to the coffee shop. Why?"

"Just trying to figure this out."

CHAPTER 37

Ashley

I couldn't eat—my stomach was doing so many flips and flops.

Hayley said, "Don't worry. Mr. Forster will get those girls for what they did."

I felt as if I were dragging myself all the way to his office. His secretary must have been at lunch, because the outer office was empty. I tapped lightly on his door.

"Come in," he said.

I pushed the door open, and there were Liz and Denise in chairs by his desk. A third chair sat empty. It was all I could do to keep from running.

"Have a seat, Ashley," Principal Forster said.

I pulled the chair a few inches away from the girls. They attempted a couple of pretty weak smiles, which I couldn't make myself return. I felt like a coward, but I wasn't about to be phony. I wished Mr. Forster had told me they were going to be here, but then I realized I would have worried about it the whole day.

"Well," Mr. Forster said in an upbeat tone, "let's get down to business. Liz, Denise, what do you have to say for yourselves?"

"About what?" Liz said.

Denise nodded. "We didn't do anything."

"About the unkind posters on the lockers and the walls?"

"What makes you think we did that?" Liz said.

Mr. Foster put his fingertips together. "Well, I was at the concert the other night and noticed the shabby start. Mr. Scarberry told me what happened and then described what went on Friday at Happy Canyons. It's obvious you two and Ashley have had your troubles."

"I wouldn't say that," Denise said, her voice dripping with sweetness. "Kids have disagreements all the time, and you know how competitive band can be." She leaned forward. "Surely you don't get involved in every little dispute."

Mr. Forster stared at her, resting his chin in his hand. "No, but I wouldn't characterize this as a little dispute. What happened at Happy Canyons was dangerous. And those posters represent a threat to one of my students."

"She started it," Liz said.

Denise gave Liz a look and she fell silent.

We all glanced at each other, then at anything *but* each other. It made me want to laugh, which wouldn't have been a good idea.

"Mr. Forster," I said finally, "can the three of us have a minute?"

He raised his eyebrows and stood. "Maybe that's a good idea."

As he closed the door, Liz and Denise looked like they'd been slapped in the face with wet eels.

Honestly, I didn't know what I was going to say. I wanted Mr. Forster to throw them out of school forever. I wanted them to go to some home for wayward girls and spend the rest of their lives making socks or license plates. I breathed a quick prayer.

"This has gone far enough," I said. "Everybody knows you hate my guts. But my guts and I can handle that. If it keeps up, though, Mr. Forster's going to call your parents, and you'll be in bigger trouble. I don't know how they punish you, but mine start taking away stuff until it hurts."

They both just stared, Liz with her mouth open.

"Why don't we try to get along," I said. "I'll forget the stuff you pulled Friday and today, Hayley won't bother you, and we'll move on."

Denise looked at Liz, then back at me. "We didn't do the signs, but okay. We'll leave you alone, and you get Forster off our backs."

I stood and held out a hand. "Deal."

That was as close to turning the other cheek as I could come. I peeked into the outer office and told Mr. Forster we'd patched up our differences.

He looked at Denise and Liz. "No problems with that?"

"Yeah, we're okay," Denise said.

"All right," Mr. Forster said. "Good work. I'm proud of you all. But any more trouble and I'm calling your parents."

CHAPTER 38

Bryce

I watched the Cubs play the second game of a doubleheader on TV while I did some homework. I'd rooted for the Cubs all my life and gone to a few games with my real dad, so watching them brought back good memories. He had always said any team could have a bad century.

I couldn't wait till the end of the season when they were coming to play the Colorado Rockies. Sam said he'd get us tickets.

Ashley rushed outside so fast that I followed without thinking. She had been so tied up with Liz and Denise that she wasn't helping with my investigation, but I was okay with that.

Hayley was getting out of the car, and her mother was already talking with Mom. ". . . and the stuff was just gone," Mrs. Henderson was saying. "It was a terrible feeling to walk in there and find all those things missing."

As Hayley and Ashley went into the house, Mrs. Henderson said, "You're getting so tall, Bryce."

I never know what to say when someone says that. Thank you doesn't seem right, but what does? I grunted and smiled and shrugged. I mean, I wasn't growing on purpose.

"Could I ask you a couple of questions about the robbery?" I said.

"Sure," she said, giving Mom a wink and a smile, the universal adult sign for "isn't this cute?"

"Can you get in your house without turning off the alarm?"

"Only by opening the door with a key."

"And who has a key?"

"Everyone in the family—both girls, my husband and I, of course, and we gave one to the neighbors in case we ever get locked out."

She told me their names, and I didn't recognize them. "They're a young couple, no kids. He lost his job a few months ago."

"Really?"

"It's put a little strain on their marriage," Mrs. Henderson said, looking at my mother and seeming to wonder if she should have told me that much. She added quickly, "The police don't seem to think they're suspects. We trust them, but you never know, I guess."

"One more thing. Have you had any car trouble lately?"

Mrs. Henderson shook her head. "Nothing out of the ordinary. We just had new tires put on and an oil change. That kind of thing."

I tried to cover my surprise. "At the Instant Oil place?"

"No, we take our cars to Carhardt's. My husband wanted to make sure it was in good shape for the trip, and they suggested new tires."

CHAPTER 39

❀ Ashley ❀

When I told Hayley what had happened in Mr. Forster's office, her eyes got as round as French horns. "We made a truce, but I can't say I actually forgave them."

Hayley rolled her eyes. "You're always so hung up on the forgiveness thing. Why don't you just let God take care of that?"

"Believe me, I want to. But Jesus teaches we should forgive others just like God has forgiven us."

And there came the glazed-eyes look again. There's just no smooth way to work Jesus into a conversation. I figured she'd change the subject, but she surprised me.

"Where's it say that?" she said.

I pulled out my Bible and felt a wave of panic. It was the first time Hayley had shown any interest after I had said the *Jesus* word. I didn't want to muff this one, but I couldn't remember where the verse was. I knew it was in the Gospels somewhere—you know, Matthew, Mark, Luke, or John—but where?

I turned to the concordance and looked up *forgive.* There were about a hundred verses listed.

"Whatever," Hayley said. "I believe you that it's in there."

"No, wait a minute. . . . Okay, here it is." I turned to the sixth chapter of Matthew. "This comes right after the Lord's Prayer. You know, 'Our Father in heaven . . .'"

"I know."

"Jesus says, 'If you forgive those who sin against you, your heavenly Father will forgive you. But if you refuse to forgive others, your Father will not forgive your sins.'"

She raised her eyebrows. "But what if the other person isn't sorry?"

I frowned. "Believe me, I've been asking the same thing. But it doesn't say anything about that. It doesn't seem to matter whether the person sees that what they've done is wrong or not. I still have to show love and forgive them or at least let go of wanting to hurt them back."

She shook her head. "I don't think I'd ever be able to do that."

"Let's just hope Liz and Denise don't try anything else." As soon as I said that, I knew it was the wrong answer. I should have said something about not having to do it on our own but letting God do it through us, but that would have sounded like a sermon. I'd done a bad job of explaining things to Hayley.

CHAPTER 40

Bryce

Sam got home while we were setting the table for dinner and plunked *The Gazette* from Colorado Springs in front of me. "Metro section," he said in his deep, gravelly voice.

I'd rather have turned to Sports, but in the Metro section I found another story about stolen items.

> Red Rock police are investigating a string of thefts reported by area residents. In the past month at least six homes have been robbed of valuables with no apparent signs of forced entry.

Yesterday police discovered Civil War artifacts belonging to Robert Gerrill of Red Rock at a pawnshop on Nevada Avenue. The items had been reported missing from Gerrill's home two weeks ago. The pawnshop owner turned the items over to police and said his young son had bought the pieces and failed to record information on the seller.

"The customer was in his twenties," the owner said. "That's all we know. We don't knowingly buy stolen goods, so this upsets me."

Robert Gerrill, 54, says the artifacts have been in his family since the 1860s. "I'm just glad we got them back."

I looked in the phone book and found Mr. Gerrill. I was scared to call him, but if I wanted to find Mrs. Watson's things, I needed to talk with him.

CHAPTER 41

❀ Ashley ❀

Bryce said having both of us there would help, just like detectives do on TV, but I figured he was just scared to go alone. We promised Mom we would be home before dark.

Spring had come in full force to Colorado. The grass was greener, the temperatures warmer, and the days were getting longer. I knew it wouldn't be long before Sam took us camping. But you don't really know if spring is here to stay until the last snow is shoveled from your driveway. I've seen it snow in June.

We rode our ATVs across the hiking trail at the north end of town, parked at the trailhead, and walked to Mr. Gerrill's.

When he came to the door I remembered him from our sixth grade class. He had talked to us about fighting in Vietnam and showed us his old uniform, which he was proud still fit. He had close-cropped white hair and long, thin arms.

His wife wiped her hands on her apron as she walked from the kitchen. "Can you stay for dinner?" she said.

Bryce thanked her and told her we had just eaten. "We won't keep you long."

"Come into the war room," Mr. Gerrill said.

He took us through a narrow hallway past the living room. A TV newscast was on, and he waved at it disgustedly and said something about "the liberal media."

In a back bedroom he had several tables full of war souvenirs. Old guns and swords hung on the wall. In a glass case he had arrowheads and musket balls and ammunition from the Revolutionary War to the war in Iraq. He had brought some of these to show us at school.

He took down a sword and held it out to Bryce and me. "This is one of the pieces they stole and sold to the pawnshop. It was worn by my great-grandfather in the battle of Vicksburg." He pointed out the craftsmanship and the name of his great grandfather etched on the handle. "It's worth a lot more in sentimental value than in actual money, but when I saw it was gone, I thought about loading all my guns and finding those thieves."

"Who do you think did it?" Bryce said.

Mr. Gerrill shook his head. "I don't know. But I know one thing: they knew what they were after. Absolutely nothing else was touched. Just the stuff from my collection."

"How many people know about your collection?"

He pointed to a frame on the wall. The newsprint had faded, but you could make out his face hovering over his treasures. "That story must be 10 years old. Either the robbers have a good memory or they knew from some other way."

"Where were you when someone got in here?" Bryce said.

"It's hard to tell. I don't take inventory every day. But it must have been when my wife and I went on an overnight up to Black Hawk. The place was shut tight, though. They had to have had a key."

Black Hawk is a small town west of Denver that draws a lot of tourists because of gambling.

"Anybody know you were going?"

He shook his head. "Just a neighbor to keep an eye on the place. But he works during the day, and I can't expect him to sit and watch our door all night. The thieves walked in like they owned the place."

"No one else has a key?"

"Nope."

I noticed a smudge on the glass case. Mr. Gerrill said he didn't know where it came from.

"One more thing," Bryce said. "Did you happen to have anything done to your car before you went to Black Hawk?"

He scratched his whiskered chin. "Now that you mention it, I had to have a new timing belt. It was at close to 200,000 miles."

"Where did you have that done?"

"Over at Carhardt's Garage. They do good work."

CHAPTER 42

Bryce

Instead of going home, we headed to Carhardt's Garage to have a look around. Ashley seemed upset about some math test, and I told her we could skip it, but she said she'd go.

I called Sam on the way and found out that the owner was Jim Carhardt, who had fixed cars in Red Rock since he was a teenager. Kind of a legend in the car-repair business. Sam said he never had a problem getting his truck fixed there.

The building was just down the street from the Toot Toot Café, and Ashley and I wanted to stop for an ice cream cone, but the sun was going down. We walked by the garage on the other side of the street and sat on a bench.

The building was made out of gray cinderblocks and looked like it had been there awhile. There were four huge garage doors in the front and back and lots of cars, trucks, and RVs jammed into the parking lot. Mechanics in gray shirts with names sewn onto their pockets worked like bees in a hive.

"What are we looking for?" Ashley said.

"A key-making machine. Everybody we've talked to has either come here or to the oil-change place before they were robbed."

"Looks like an awful lot of candidates are here," she said.

I pulled out Sam's minitelescope and scanned the inside of the garage. There were lots of tools and machines of every sort, but I couldn't find what I was looking for.

Ashley poked me on the shoulder. "Recognize him?"

It was Mr. Morris, the alpaca owner.

We crossed the street. He was still inside the waiting area talking with someone when we joined him. "Ashley, Bryce!" His face lit up, and he turned to the man behind the counter. "These are the two helpers for my herd I was telling you about, Jim."

The man smiled at us. He had grimy hands and tired eyes, like he'd been up late the night before. His face was pudgy and his sideburns long, like an Elvis impersonator.

Mr. Morris waved and said he had to go. "You'll be at my place tomorrow morning, right?"

"We'll be there," Ashley said.

"How can I help you two?" Mr. Carhardt said.

"I was wondering if you guys made keys. You know, for extra house keys, that kind of thing."

"Actually we don't."

"Are you sure?

"Yeah, I own the place and we don't make keys. You can have

them made down at the hardware store, and there's a bunch of places in the Springs."

I looked at Ashley in disbelief.

"Is that all?" he said.

I had a hundred questions, none of which I could think of at the moment.

"Did you expect them to just fall down and say they were guilty?" Ashley said as we walked back to our ATVs.

"I don't know what I expected. I thought we'd find their key-making machine at least. Maybe this whole thing has nothing to do with the repair shop."

CHAPTER 43

❀ Ashley ❀

I was up first Wednesday morning, ate my breakfast, and got ready to go to the farm. Bryce rolled out of bed slower, but he has a way of throwing his clothes on, inhaling his breakfast, and beating me to the ATVs.

The grass was wet with dew when we drove to the farm, but it felt like we had almost slipped the surly bonds of school. *Two more days!* I chanted as we rolled along the field.

Mr. Morris was at the barn, waving and smiling. Buck met us, his tail wagging. Two of the boys were in the car already, and another was on the porch at the house.

"We thought you'd be gone by now," I said.

"We had some packing issues," Mr. Morris said. "I figured it wouldn't hurt to give you a few last-minute instructions." He seemed pleased that we were both there on time.

We went inside the barn. Whitney, the pregnant alpaca, strutted back and forth in her stall. She looked at us nervously and hummed.

"It's okay, girl," Mr. Morris said. "You're gonna be just fine." He faced us. "These are smart animals. She can tell something's up."

"Will it hurt her not to have you around?" Bryce said.

"She'll probably get so used to you two she won't want me to come back. Just talk in nice tones and reassure her that everything's gonna be all right."

Mr. Morris showed us a new feed trough and a scoop he had bought so it wouldn't be confusing for us to measure the pellets. "One more thing before I go." He grabbed some tools and wire and led us into the field. Most of the alpacas followed us like pups, trotting along behind. They seemed interested in everything.

Buck ran ahead of us and sniffed and pawed at a mangled spot in the fence.

"Just found this earlier while I was making my morning rounds." Mr. Morris picked up two twisted ends of wire from the ground. "If I had to guess, I'd say it was a bear. You can still smell the thing, and there are droppings a few yards that way."

My heart raced with the news. "Do they usually come at night like that?"

"They eat any time they're hungry, which is all the time. But a lot of people find their trash cans overturned in the middle of the night. I'm just glad the thing didn't get to any of the animals."

He showed us how to mend the fence. I was glad Bryce was there because he's better at that kind of thing. The car horn honked, and Mr. Morris chuckled. "The kids can't wait to get on the road."

When he was finished, he showed us where he kept the tools and walked toward the house. "Now I meant it when I said you two are welcome to stay at the house overnight. You can stay here the whole week if you'd like."

Bryce smiled. "We hope Sam and Mom will let us."

We helped them load their car and waved as they drove away. Bryce looked at his watch. "I forgot my backpack. I need to go home and get it before we head to school."

"I'll meet you at Mrs. Watson's place," I said. "I just want to stay here a little longer."

Bryce took off, and I walked among the alpacas. There was something peaceful about being with this many animals, and with Buck patrolling the edge of the pasture, I felt safe.

A bear, I thought. *What if the bear comes back when we're gone? What if it comes back when we're here?*

I went back inside the barn and looked at Whitney. I tried to soothe her a little with my words, but it didn't work. She looked through the cracks in the barn and hummed louder.

I made sure all the gates were closed and the animals had enough food and water. When I got to the end of the driveway I closed the main gate behind me.

A car came barreling past me, kicking up dust. I flipped my helmet visor down just in time to recognize Denise in the backseat. She scowled as she passed, but I wasn't sure she knew who I was.

I let the dust settle, then followed down the road to the field where I would cut across and head to school. I looked back once and saw most of the herd standing at the edge of the pasture. It was almost like they were saying good-bye.

CHAPTER 44

Bryce

At lunch I told my friends about our alpaca project.

Duncan still seemed miffed at me for Happy Canyons, but he sat with me and some of the other guys. "How much they gonna pay you to do all that work?" he said.

"We never talked about pay."

"My mom paid one of our neighbors $100 just to walk our dog and feed our old cat," Kael said. "I told her I would have stayed home and done it for half that much."

"How many alpacas do they have?" Duncan said.

"About 40."

"And they'll be gone a whole week?"

"Yeah, why?"

"That could be some serious money. Let's say they give you $2 an alpaca every day. That's $80 a day. And 80 times 7—"

"$560," Skeeter said. "You and Ashley are rich!"

"And that's if they only give you $2 per animal," Duncan said. "You need any help?"

I couldn't help smiling. I hadn't thought much about the payment, but Duncan made quite a case. "I think Ashley and I can handle it."

Toby came to the table and sat down.

Duncan excused himself—too quickly.

"Bryce, you know you were talking about people having stuff stolen?" Toby said. "I met another kid whose parents came back from vacation last week, and the same thing happened to them."

"Who is it?"

"Come on. I'll introduce you."

CHAPTER 45

❀ Ashley ❀

We got our tests back in math, and my score was miserable. The only good thing was that most people—other than Marion Quidley—did just as poorly, and the teacher had mercy on us. I squeaked through with a B for the class, but just barely.

I saw Denise in the hall once, but she didn't notice me. I wasn't half as worried about her and Liz as I was about the alpacas. I hoped they'd be okay.

At lunch I saw Bryce talking with Duncan. A few minutes later,

Bryce motioned for me to follow him. He and Toby went to the back where a scrawny-looking kid was eating lunch.

"This is Bryce and Ashley," Toby said to the kid. "Stan, tell them what you told me about your parents' house."

"There's not much to tell," Stan said. "We had to go out of town for a funeral. When we got back, all my mom's expensive silverware was gone, plus her jewelry. They also got a few coins my dad had kept to give us kids. Some of them were worth thousands."

"Did the thieves break in?" Bryce said.

"No, it was almost like they walked into the place without any problem. Like they had a key or something."

"Who died?" I said.

Bryce scrunched his face. "What?"

"The funeral—who was it for?" I said.

"Oh, an uncle of mine," Stan said, biting his cheek. "Lived in Oregon. He had a car accident."

"I'm sorry. Must've been really hard to go through that and then come back to having stuff taken from your house."

"Yeah, Mom cried about it for days. Dad was spittin' mad, but what could he do? What can any of us do?"

"Have the police said anything?" Bryce said.

"They don't give us much hope. Maybe they'll catch the people one day. I hope so."

"One more question," Bryce said. "Did your dad get his car fixed before the trip?"

Stan took a bite of his apple and shook his head. "We got the call in the evening on Tuesday. Then we left for the airport early the next day. There wasn't time to get anything worked on."

I walked with Bryce to his locker. He shook his head. "I was sure this all had to do with the repair shop or the oil change place."

"Maybe the thieves don't use keys," I said. "On some of those TV shows they can get into houses without them, and it still looks like they didn't force their way in."

"In that case it could be anybody."

"We can't give up," I said. "We have to keep following the leads until we find something. Talk to Stan's parents. Something will turn up."

CHAPTER 46

◎ *Bryce* ◎

Ashley and I went to the farm as soon as school was out and made sure the alpacas were okay. Buck was there waiting for us, wagging his tail. I checked on his food and water and made sure Lewis, the parrot, had food. He squawked at me when I opened the cage and said, "Thank you for calling."

I went to the mangled fence and saw that it was still in good shape. No more repairs needed. "We need you to be on the alert tonight," I said to Buck, patting his head. "You take good care of these animals and yourself."

It almost felt like Buck understood. He panted and looked at me for a long time, then trotted off through the pasture. He stopped about midway to the barn, his ears pointing up, hair bristling. He gave a low growl and looked toward the woods beyond the house, then continued to the barn.

When we got home, both Ashley and I were starved. I think it's working outside that does it, but I felt like I could eat everything in the refrigerator—including the plain yogurt Mom eats. Mom made us wait, saying Sam would be home soon. When he didn't come, she let us start.

Sam finally came in and apologized, saying he had had trouble with his truck coming from the airport. "Gotta take it into the shop. First time they can see it is early Friday morning."

"You can take my car tomorrow," Mom said.

He nodded, and I looked at Ashley. I didn't know exactly what we were going to do, but it seemed like the perfect chance to get more information.

Later in Ashley's room, she came up with the plan. "You hide in the backseat of Sam's truck. He'll think you're at the farm already or sleeping in after the last day of school. When he leaves it, you stay out of sight and just listen, see if you hear anything."

"What if Mom asks about me?"

"I'll cover for you. Should be easy since we've got the alpacas. I'll just say you're working on something."

"What if the people at the repair shop find me?"

She shrugged. "I'll speak at your funeral."

We both laughed. Then she scooted closer. "Look, this will either confirm your suspicion or let you move on to some other theory."

CHAPTER 47

Ashley

There's a feeling you get on the last day of school that's like no other. Especially the last day of seventh grade. You know you have all of eighth grade ahead of you, all of the rest of middle school behind you, and all of being called pixie and newbie out of the way. When you're an eighth grader, you're only one step away from high school, and that commands respect.

Bryce and I fed the animals. They all seemed okay, though Whitney looked skittish when we approached. We gave her some food and tried to stay out of her way.

We flew through the field and made it to school in record time, though riding through some tall grass really got our legs wet. It felt good to wear shorts on the last day since our classes were basically over, and all that was left was to hand in our books, clean out our lockers, and say good-bye.

At lunch there was a lot of free food—the cooks were cleaning out their kitchen—and Mr. Forster had a pie-throwing competition. For a dollar you could throw a whipped-cream pie at the gym teachers wearing plastic ponchos, and all the money went back to the school.

We had a band get-together at lunch and said good-bye to the eighth grade band members. Liz and Denise stayed to themselves, but at one point, Liz walked over to me. "Don't think this is over, Timberline," she said.

It was all I needed to decide to quit the band. I didn't want to spend the summer worrying about next year. I knew it was a shame just to throw my flute away, but I'd had enough.

CHAPTER 48

◎ *Bryce* ◎

The most fun part of the day was when Mr. Forster went onto the football field and we all lined up for a chance to knock him in the dunk tank. There must have been 20 people who failed, with Mr. Forster taunting them, before Duncan sailed a fastball into the center of the target and everybody whooped. Mr. Forster went into the tank like a rock and came up sputtering and laughing.

I dunked Mr. Scarberry, our band director. He stayed under the water and raised his baton above the surface. It was pretty funny.

The cooks came outside and cheered the kids on. Several even bought chances to sink teachers and administrators. Mrs. Garcia, the Lunch Lady, missed the target by a mile but ran up and smacked the lever with her hand, sending the assistant principal into the drink.

By the time the last bell rang, girls were crying and hugging teachers they couldn't stand the rest of the year. Others sniffled as they signed yearbooks. I couldn't understand it. We were going to see all of these people in a couple of months, except for the eighth graders, and to be honest, I was glad they were leaving.

The one person noticeably absent was Boo Heckler.

I sidled up to Duncan and put an arm around him, and he smiled. I figured by the time of our first sleepover the whole stolen-items caper would be over and I could tell him why I hadn't chosen him as my buddy at Happy Canyons. Then everything would be back to normal.

"So, where do you suppose Boo is?" I said.

Duncan stepped back quickly. "You haven't heard? He got sent to juvenile hall for doing something to mailboxes. And he has to repeat eighth grade next fall. I hear he's pretty ticked and looking for whoever ratted him out."

No one but the police knew it was Ashley and me.

"I can't imagine next year with Boo in our classes," Duncan said.

Unfortunately, I could.

CHAPTER 49

✱ Ashley ✱

I couldn't breathe when Bryce told me about Boo Heckler. I felt sorry for his teachers.

Everything looked okay with the alpacas. I collected the Morrises' paper and mail and put them in the house, then joined Bryce in the garage. We filled Buck's food bowl.

When we went back outside smoke was coming from Denise's yard. A couple of cars were parked outside, and people were setting up a volleyball net.

"Looks like a party," Bryce said. "You should go see what's for dinner."

"I should send Buck," I said.

As we mounted up to head home, I said, "You sure you're going to be all right in that truck tomorrow? It could get hot."

"Already figured that out. I have water bottles in the freezer. Gonna move them to the truck before morning."

"How are you going to get up in time?"

"I'm going to sleep in the truck under a blanket. Sam will never even see me."

CHAPTER 50

Bryce

I waited until everyone had been in bed a couple of hours before I grabbed my favorite blanket, my empty backpack, and my cell phone and crept downstairs to the refrigerator. Every second I was sure I was being too loud and that Sam or Mom would come investigate.

I filled the bottom of the backpack with the frozen water bottles, then put in some apples, a couple of sandwiches, two candy bars, and some small bags of chips from the pantry. It wasn't until I was outside that I could breathe again.

Sam had left the truck windows down, and it was chilly. I stowed my stuff under his seat and stretched out on the backseat. I could have turned the key halfway and closed the windows, but he kept the keys on the dresser in the master bedroom, and I wasn't about to risk sneaking in there. It was so cold that I wished I'd brought my sleeping bag. I set my phone on vibrate, then tossed and turned the whole night. I guess I slept some, but it didn't feel like it.

The sun was almost up when I heard the front door. I scooted onto the floor behind the front seat and made sure I was covered. Sam got in, closed the door, and burped. I had to clamp my hand over my mouth to keep from laughing.

Sam drove toward town, keeping the windows down the whole way. He finally stopped and got out. I stayed still as a statue, then peeked over the back of the seat. We were in front of one of the garage doors at Carhardt's. Sam was inside talking with the owner. When he headed back out, I ducked again and heard a familiar honk behind me. It had to be Mom picking him up.

I'm in!

CHAPTER 51

❀ Ashley ❀

As soon as I woke up, I called Bryce's cell phone. The phone picked up, but he didn't say anything. A few seconds later he whispered, "That you, Ash?"

"Where are you?"

"Still in the truck. Sam just left with Mom. There's a guy coming—hang on."

My heart pounded. I imagined someone mistaking Bryce for a thief. A door closed. The truck started.

"Bryce, get out of there," I said.

The phone crackled as Bryce moved. Then I heard a door close.

“Okay, he’s gone,” Bryce said. “He just backed into the parking lot. And he put the windows up.”

“It’s gonna get hot in there.”

He told me it would be a nice change from a cold night.

I clicked on the computer weather channel. “Supposed to hit 80 degrees today.”

“Ugh. Unless I can get some air, I might need to bail.”

“Call me at the farm if you need me,” I said.

CHAPTER 52

Bryce

Sam's truck had tinted windows, so that blocked some of the heat. Best of all, I could peer out at names on guys' shirts without their seeing me.

When things started heating up I took a drink from one of my water bottles. I started feeling short of breath, so I climbed into the front seat and turned the key until it beeped. Then I rolled down the front windows a few inches. The wind made a nice breeze through the truck.

Twenty minutes later a sandy-haired guy whose name tag read Eddie jogged to the truck. I hunkered down as he jumped in and pulled into the garage.

Guys yelled to each other over the country music blaring on the radio. Somebody reached in and popped the hood. I listened to the *clink* and *clank* of hammers, the *brrrrrfffffftttt* of some tire machine, and the *clunk-clunk-clunk* of the oil pump.

I peeked at my watch. Ashley would be at the farm by now, but I didn't dare call her. Someone might hear me.

I tried to match voices with names. One guy talked about fishing and camping trips, another about an old car he was fixing. The owner came in every now and then to check on people's work. They all seemed to know what they were doing.

Could any of these guys really be robbing people in Red Rock? Who would steal in the same town he worked in? He'd have to be awfully dumb or really bold.

My phone vibrated. The readout showed it was Ashley, but there was no way I could talk now.

Someone phoned Sam, told him what they'd found wrong with the truck, and said they'd have to keep it overnight.

Great. How am I going to get home?

CHAPTER 53

❀ Ashley ❀

I called Bryce from inside the Morrises' house and got his voice mail, so I figured he would call me when he could.

"We'll be right back after these messages!" Lewis squawked, startling me.

Then I heard something weird, like someone was banging on a nail. I looked out the back window, wondering if someone was building a house.

Nothing.

When I opened the front door I realized it wasn't pounding but Buck barking, sharp and loud. I raced to the barn but found it empty except for Whitney, who was pacing again, peering through the slats, and humming.

"Where's the rest of the herd, Whitney?" I said, and I would have hardly been surprised if she had told me.

I could hear Buck down the driveway, so I ran out, only to find an ambulance parked outside the gate. A paramedic was talking to a girl in a robe.

I ran closer. "Denise!"

CHAPTER 54

Bryce

The garage phone rang every few minutes, and the radio got on my nerves. The music made it hard to hear the conversations.

Someone called out, "Hey, lover boy!" Other guys laughed. "Eddie?" the man said in a singsong voice. "Phone call. It's your sweetheart."

I peeked over the seat and through the slit between the hood and the truck frame. The man handed a greasy cordless phone to Eddie, who hopped into Sam's truck and closed the door. I had slid out of sight just in time.

"Yeah, hang on," he said. "Let me close the windows." The others hooted at him and clapped. "Okay, what happened?"

Eddie chuckled. "Perfect. Good girl. Way to go. Where are you now? . . . You're kidding, that close? . . . What happened?"

He paused.

"Okay, stay there and make sure they take him away."

Another pause.

"Well, the next step is to get the trailer . . . no, not till tomorrow, so it'll be tomorrow night."

I couldn't make sense of what he was talking about, but it sure didn't seem to have anything to do with Mrs. Watson's stolen stuff.

"Okay, don't let anybody see you," Eddie said. "Call in sick, tell them what happened . . . no, don't let them make you go to the doctor. . . . Do you know how much those are worth? We'll be able to blow this town before anybody suspects. Our dreams come true Saturday night."

CHAPTER 55

❀ Ashley ❀

I flew down the gravel driveway so fast that I almost lost my footing. Denise was wearing a bathing suit under the terry cloth robe, and she'd been crying.

"What happened?" I said.

"It was awful," Denise cried. "I saw the whole thing."

"What? Tell me!"

The paramedic stepped toward me. "You own that dog?"

Buck's pure white coat was streaked with blood.

"What happened to him?" I said.

"Ma'am, your dog attacked a jogger."

"What? Buck's not my dog, but he wouldn't—"

"Is the owner here?"

"They're on vacation. I'm watching the farm. Will somebody please—?"

A silver sheriff's car roared up, lights whirling and leather creaking when an officer got out.

A sob welled up inside me as I moved toward Buck. He was on the other side of the fence with a few alpacas around him, as if they were the ones guarding him.

"Miss, you need to stay away from that animal," the officer said.

I heard a snap and saw him draw his gun. "No! Don't shoot him!"

"I'm not going to shoot unless he attacks. Now stand back."

I burst into tears. "He doesn't attack people."

"He did today," the paramedic said.

"Who?"

"That's classified."

Buck growled. I yelled at him to stop and he did, his tongue hanging as he panted.

The officer wrote down my information. "Animal control is on the way," he said.

"What for? Buck's not going to hurt anyone."

"We're going to make sure of that," the officer said. "We'll keep him quarantined. Do you know if his shots are up to date?"

I shrugged. "He's got those things on his collar, and Mr. Morris says he has all his animals vaccinated every year."

"So this is the Morris place, huh? You have a phone number for him?"

"In the house. But I don't think his cell works where they are."

"I'll need it anyway."

I hesitated, looking at Buck.

"He'll still be here when you get back."

CHAPTER 56

Bryce

Eddie got out of the truck and closed the door. The windows were up again, which blocked some of the garage smells, but I couldn't hear much except the tinny music.

"Lunch!" somebody called.

The whole garage emptied and I was glad. I lowered the windows again, then called Ashley. If you're wondering why she doesn't have a cell phone, Mom said we had to pay for them. I had the cash but Ashley didn't.

The phone rang at the farm until the answering machine picked up. I hung up and dialed our home number. Mom answered and asked how everything at the farm was going.

"Fine, I guess. . . . Hey, Ashley's not there, is she?"

"She's not with you?"

"Well, she's probably in the barn. I'll find her."

"Bryce, what's going on?"

"Nothing. Can you do me a favor?" I asked her to look up Stan's phone number from the school directory.

She gave it to me and said, "Now tell me what's up."

"Mom, it's detective stuff. We're fine. I'll see you later."

I called the farm again. No answer. I dialed Stan's and he picked up.

"Double-checking, Stan. Are you sure your dad didn't take his car to the repair shop before your trip to Oregon?"

"He's right here. Let me ask."

Stan came back on. "We were going on a trip this week. Dad had an appointment at Carhardt's, but he canceled it."

Then how did the robbers get the key?

"Any other work on the car around that time?" I said.

Stan covered the phone again. Then, "Nothing but an oil change."

"At Carhardt's?"

"No. He always goes to Instant Oil."

CHAPTER 57

Ashley

When I got back a white van had pulled up and a lady in a blue uniform was talking with the officer and the paramedic. She was tall and thin and looked like one of those beach volleyball players, her hair pulled back under a baseball cap. She wore dark, wraparound sunglasses.

I whispered to Denise, "Do you know who the jogger was?"

"I've seen her before, but I can't remember where."

"Is she in the ambulance?"

Denise shook her head. "She limped off. Said she didn't want any treatment but that somebody should take care of that dog."

"I can't imagine Buck attacking anyone."

"He did," Denise said. "I was out by our pool when I heard the barking. I didn't think much of it because that dog barks a lot. Then I heard screaming. I threw on my robe and ran down here. He just attacked her as she was running. She had bite marks and blood on her legs. I don't know how she walked away."

"You actually saw the attack?"

"You bet I did. And I wouldn't want anybody else to get bitten like that. Look at him. They say once a dog tastes human blood, he wants more."

The officer came over. "Ashley, we're going to take the animal." The way he said *animal* made it sound like *murderer.*

"But we need him! He protects the herd!"

Buck growled again as the animal control lady joined us. "He was probably just scared," she said. "Something about the jogger frightened him, and he probably thought he was protecting his herd, like you say. But we have to check him out, make sure nothing's wrong, okay?"

I nodded, but it wasn't okay. "Where are you taking him?"

"To the shelter. Until . . . we figure out what to do next."

She went to her truck and brought out a long pole with a rope at the end.

"Wait," I said. "You don't have to use that."

The officer waved. "We can't let you—"

"Buck won't hurt you. He's nice. I'll show you."

Before they could stop me I crawled through the fence and knelt by Buck. I have to admit he had a wild look, like something wasn't right. I reached to pet him and he growled.

"That's it!" the officer shouted, drawing his gun again. "Get away from him!"

"It's okay," I whispered to Buck. "I'm not going to let anything happen to you. I promise."

Buck whined and turned, licking my hand. I patted his head and scratched under his chin, and he bounced up and ran around the alpacas. They were all restless and humming.

"Don't let him get away!" the officer said.

"Put your gun away and I'll bring him over," I said. "Where do you want him?"

The lady pointed to the side door of her van. The officer and Denise stepped behind the sheriff's cruiser. I crawled back through the fence and patted my knees, coaxing Buck to follow. He loped after me. I stepped into the van where a cage separated the driver from the back and smaller cages were stacked. Buck followed me inside, then whined as if sensing something wrong.

Before I knew it the door closed behind me, and a smaller door opened on the other side.

"Ashley, hurry!" the woman said.

I jumped out before Buck could follow. He scratched at the door, then started barking louder than I had ever heard him. I heard cages tumbling as he lunged at the back window, leaving streaks of blood on it.

"That's one vicious dog," the officer said.

CHAPTER 58

Bryce

There had to be some connection between Instant Oil and Carhardt's. I was convinced Eddie was involved—maybe copying house keys from people's car key rings. All I had to do was prove it. If the police searched Eddie's home, they were sure to find Mrs. Watson's jewelry as well as stuff from the other houses.

I opened my first sandwich and ate it in about five bites. The chips were salty and good—I ate two bags fast. The water had almost melted completely, and I drank the rest of my first bottle.

I dialed the farmhouse again. Ashley must have been out with the alpacas. I sure hoped she hadn't run into that bear.

A door banged and the mechanics returned. I settled back under my cover. I was so close to the floor I could see under Sam's front seat. There were empty water bottles and food wrappers, plus a lot of dust. Before I could stifle it, I sneezed.

"Bless you, Eddie," somebody said.

"That wasn't me," he said.

CHAPTER 59

❀ Ashley ❀

Denise was still there when the officer, the animal control lady, and the ambulance pulled away.

"Where did the girl go?" I said.

Denise scowled. "I told you, back down the road, that way."

"But there aren't any houses there. And I don't see any trail of blood."

She shrugged. "She just said she didn't want the paramedic treating her. But she gave her number to the guy and said she'd have her dad call to make sure they put the dog away."

"You mean kill him?"

"The cop said they'd have to if they couldn't get hold of the owner."

"What!?"

Denise shook her head. "I'm sorry about the dog, but there's no way they can let that thing run loose."

"I have to find that girl. You sure you don't know who she is?"

"Maybe a high schooler. Could be in college. I don't know."

I ran full tilt back to the barn and hopped on my ATV. By the time I roared to the road and shut the gate, Denise was gone. I was kicking up so much dust I decided to get off the road and into a field near some pine trees. The mountain loomed to my left and a cow pasture to my right.

Where could the girl have gone? I scanned the horizon. Near the access road off the interstate about half a mile away, someone ran toward a small car. I gunned it toward the road and tried to catch up, but the car pulled out in a cloud of dust and raced away.

CHAPTER 60

Bryce

I held my breath as the guys tried to find who had sneezed. Finally someone turned the radio back on, and I felt relieved. I wondered what would happen if I just got out and walked to the waiting room and then outside. I could hoof it to Mrs. Watson's, and Ashley could come get me, if I ever got hold of her.

Eddie said something about the exhaust system, and suddenly the truck rose several feet. My heart raced when I looked out the window. It felt like I was 10 feet off the ground. No way was I going to jump that far.

I could see out a window at the top of the garage as the sun traced across the sky. I wondered if Mom was worried. Maybe Ashley was already home and trying to cover for me. I tried the farm again, but there was no answer.

I could hear Eddie under the car. "Hey, we still on for the horse trailer? Remember I was hoping to borrow it this weekend?"

"Why don't you just use your truck?"

"I need more space. Now can I use it?"

The other guy paused. "I don't think my dad needs it."

"Good. I'll pick it up tomorrow morning before work if that's okay."

CHAPTER 61

❀ Ashley ❀

I called Bryce as soon as I got back to the farmhouse. He picked up but didn't even whisper. "Call when you can talk," I said.

"When you can talk," Lewis said.

"Shut up, bird."

"Shut up, bird!" Lewis squawked.

While I was making myself a sandwich, Bryce finally called and told me what he'd heard.

"How do they get the keys?" I said.

"I'm not sure yet, but I know they're planning a big heist tomorrow night."

"Where?"

"I don't know that either, but—"

"Bryce, remember we saw Mr. Morris there, talking to the owner about going out of town. Could the big heist be here?"

I heard clanging in the background, like someone had dropped a tool. Finally Bryce whispered, "Could be. We have to catch them."

I told Bryce about Buck. He couldn't believe it. "I guess animal control can't take any chances," he said, "but how are we going to protect the herd in the meantime?"

"We have no choice. We'll have to do it ourselves and stay here overnight. When are you coming back?"

"That's up in the air right now—literally."

"I'll come and get you," I said.

"No, go home and wait. I'll meet you there. If I'm not there by dinner, call me."

CHAPTER 62

Bryce

Ashley and I couldn't leave the alpacas alone—especially at night—as long as Buck was away.

What if we did save their lives? Would Mr. Morris pay more? What if he gave us $5 an alpaca each day? I did the math on my watch calculator. Ashley and I would both get $700!

I knew it was wrong to think that way. I had to do a good job whether or not we were paid at all.

The longer I lay in the pickup, the more cramped my legs felt. I wanted to sleep, but I had to stay alert. I wondered what Ashley would tell Mom when she showed up at home without me.

CHAPTER 63

❀ Ashley ❀

When I got home I went straight to Sam's office above the barn. I didn't want to face Mom because I knew she'd ask me where Bryce was, and I wasn't going to lie.

Sam's office is really cool. There's a weight/exercise room on one end, where Bryce and I work out and play video games. On the other end is Sam's office with a desk, file cabinets, and pictures of planes. Sometimes I go there just to think. Maybe the smell of coffee gets my mind going—it smells like one of those big bookstores we go to in Colorado Springs.

I couldn't find anything that would scare off bears, mountain lions, or coyotes. Maybe something that made noise would work. A fire would keep them away—we had done that while camping.

Suddenly the intercom crackled to life. "Ashley, Bryce, are you over there?"

"I'm here, Mom."

"Would you and Bryce get in here, please?"

Of course, as soon as I got inside, she said, "Where's Bryce?"

"Around," I said, sticking my head in the fridge. "What's for dinner?"

Mom had a hand on her hip when I turned around. "What's going on? I haven't seen you two all day."

I wanted to tell her all about Buck and Bryce, but I just shrugged and gave her my best laid-back answer. "Mom, it's an alpaca thing."

I could tell she wasn't buying it. When she found out about everything, we'd have a lot of explaining to do, but that could wait.

I spotted Leigh's key chain on the counter. She'd just gotten her driver's license, and Sam had bought her a fancy chain with something attached.

"What's this?" I said, holding it up.

"It's spray Mace. Don't ever touch that. It can blind people temporarily, and it's only to be used if Leigh is attacked."

"How close do you have to be?"

"It sprays something like 15 feet, but don't—"

"I know. I know. I won't use it on Dylan. Though I could have used it with Denise and Liz."

She smiled. I could tell she wanted to talk. I ran for the front door.

"Where are you going now?"

"To check on Mrs. Watson."

CHAPTER 64

Bryce

I woke up as the truck shook and realized it had been lowered. Someone got in and started the engine.

I couldn't believe I had fallen asleep. My body felt like a pretzel, and my mouth tasted like pennies. The guy got out and shut the door. I threw the cover off and sat up. My arm looked like I had a tattoo. It was covered with lines and dots from the floor, plus I had drool all over my cheek. I hate when that happens.

Just as I was about to make my move, Eddie reached for the door and I had to lie back down. He reached in and turned the engine off.

The phone rang, and the owner stuck his head into the garage. "Lover boy, it's for you again. You've reached your quota."

"Yes, sir," Eddie said. He returned with the cordless phone, sat in the pickup, and rolled up the windows. "You make it out of there? . . . Good. What about the—? . . . You sure, 'cause I'm not going into that place with—"

Eddie seemed more and more excited. "Okay, good. You gave them the right name? . . . All right, on break I'll call them from a pay phone and chew them out, tell them I want him taken care of." He lowered his voice and acted like he was older. Then he laughed. "Hey, we're almost home free. This'll be our last gig and you can finally tell your mom to shove it."

I was relieved when he was finally out of the truck again. I had been wrong before, jumped to conclusions about people, so I tried to think of anything he could be talking about that didn't involve stealing. "Our last gig" made me think of music—could he be part of a band? Maybe the trailer was for hauling amps and equipment.

I was hot, tired, and ready to get out of here. It was getting hard to breathe again, but how could I slip out without anyone seeing me?

"Excuse me?" someone said. "I need to get in my dad's truck."

Ashley.

"I left something in there. Can I—?"

"Sure," Eddie said, "go ahead."

Ashley climbed inside. "You still alive?" she whispered.

"Barely."

"I'll cause a diversion in the waiting area. When you hear me scream, get out of here."

Ashley took some papers from the glove compartment and got out. I sat up and got ready. Seconds later Ashley screamed, and the mechanics rushed toward the sound.

I jumped out and crab walked out of the garage to the parking lot. I leaned against a tree, finally able to breathe.

Ashley came out of the waiting room, brushing off her shirt and smiling.

"What'd you do in there?" I said.

"You know that big stack of tires? It's kind of not there anymore. Clumsy me."

"Thanks," I said. "I could've been stuck there all night."

We crossed the street and hurried toward Mrs. Watson's house where Ashley had parked her ATV. I stopped short.

Ashley turned. "What?"

I put my head down and kept walking. Eddie was on the other side of the road watching us.

CHAPTER 65

❈ Ashley ❈

I kept complimenting Mom on how tasty everything was at dinner until Bryce kicked me under the table. I guess he thought I was overdoing it, especially in front of Dylan and Leigh.

"Mom?" Bryce said. "What would you think about Ashley and me sleeping at the Morrises' tonight? Mr. Morris said he wanted us to."

"Can I go too?" Dylan said.

Mom shook her head. "Not with Sam gone. I don't want you out there alone. That big dog you told me about can take care of the alpacas tonight."

I was desperate to persuade her without telling what had happened to Buck, and I especially didn't want to say anything about the evidence of a bear. Bryce seemed at a loss for words too.

"Let them go," Leigh said. "If there's a problem, I'll go get them."

It was like someone had opened a window on a hot day, turned on a fan, and handed me a frosty glass of lemonade. Leigh had never jumped in for us like that, and I could tell Mom was just as surprised.

She sat back and studied Bryce and Leigh and me. "Well, if Leigh will pinch-hit for Sam, I guess it's okay."

"And tomorrow night too," Bryce said, jumping up and taking his plate to the sink. "They have satellite, and it's like 50 times clearer than our cable."

"We'll see," Mom said.

"But it's the Cubs and the Cardinals at Wrigley."

"We'll see, I said."

CHAPTER 66

Bryce

The alpacas seemed more jumpy than usual, probably because they missed Buck.

Ashley kept looking at Denise's house and then the road. "I still say he didn't attack her," she said.

"Wasn't there blood all over?"

"Yeah, but just in one spot. Don't you think if she had really been bitten, she would have left a trail? And if Buck thought she was a threat, why didn't he kill her? Why did he stop, and how did she call the paramedics?"

"I thought Denise called them," I said. "If the jogger was just making this up, how did she know anyone would be watching?"

"Maybe she waited until she saw someone outside at Denise's."

"But why, Ash?" I said. "What would be the point?"

She shrugged. "What if someone was trying to get Buck out of here so they could rob the house? Otherwise they'd have to kill him or the neighbors would hear the barking."

I snapped my fingers. "None of the places that were robbed had a dog. Mrs. Watson took hers with her."

"How would the burglars know?"

"They probably check the places out first."

It was getting dark, so we made sure all the alpacas were in the barn. Whitney was still walking back and forth.

The phone was ringing when we got back inside. It was Mom. "Mr. Morris called a few minutes ago and said he wasn't able to reach you. He asked how things were going. I told him you were staying there tonight, and he seemed happy about that. He said he'd call again Sunday or Monday. Everything all right out there?"

I heard a yip and a howl, and the hair on the back of my neck stood on end. "Yeah, great."

CHAPTER 67

✾ Ashley ✾

Bryce quickly dialed the Morrises' cell phone, hoping they would still be in range, but he got their voice mail. He asked them to call and said it was urgent.

I called animal control. There wasn't much chance of reaching anyone there on a Friday evening, but it was worth a try. No luck.

I looked up the number for the sheriff's office and handed the phone to Bryce. He had found ice cream in the freezer and looked at the phone like it was a dead skunk.

"Ask the officer what they're going to do with Buck," I said.

He poured a glop of chocolate syrup on the ice cream. "Mr. Morris will call and work it out."

"That could be too late. I have a bad feeling."

He put a big spoonful in his mouth. "Call him yourself. You're the one who talked to him." He walked into the living room, flipped on a sports channel, and plopped onto the sofa.

"Bryce, this is serious!"

A recap of the Cubs game flashed on the screen, and I knew I'd lost him.

I dialed the nonemergency number, and an operator told me the officer I had talked to was not on duty. After I explained the problem, she suggested I call animal control Monday.

"But that could be too late."

"Best I can do is to connect you with Officer Tolson's voice mailbox."

I spilled my story in the message and said, "If they might put Buck down if they can't get hold of the Morrises, please don't let that happen. They'll be back within phone range Sunday. At least call me before anything happens, please!"

I couldn't watch baseball replays, so I stood in the kitchen looking out the window at Denise's house. Lights lit her back patio, and I could make out a couple of people sitting there.

"I'm going out for a couple of minutes," I said.

Bryce grunted.

The distance between the Morris farm and Denise's house was about two football fields and filled with tall grass. I went slow, keeping an eye on the house while trying to avoid any holes. I finally climbed through the fence to Denise's property and drew close enough to hear voices. It was Denise and Liz. They had a small fire going in a pit near the swimming pool.

CHAPTER 68

Bryce

The Cubs had lost to the Cardinals by a run in the ninth inning on a wild pitch. I wanted to throw my ice cream at the television. I couldn't wait until Saturday night to see them get revenge. The two teams have been rivals almost since David and Goliath.

I flipped the TV off. It was dark out now, and the moon rose full above the pine trees on the mountain behind us. Everything seemed peaceful.

"Ash?" I called. *Hmm. Still out. Where was she going?*

"We'll be right back after these messages," Lewis squawked.

I almost had a heart attack. He scared me every time. I covered his cage and went outside. Immediately I heard a low, guttural sound, like someone breathing heavily.

"Ashley?" I called, knowing it couldn't be her.

Then I smelled it—stale, rancid, like rotten food mixed with barn smells. There and then gone with the breeze.

I walked farther into the yard and looked at the barn. Dew had begun to form and glistened in the moonlight—a soft, shimmering light like you see on lakes and the ocean.

Something moved in the distance. A black dot bobbed along the hill, just outside the fence line. Was it my imagination? a cloud moving in front of the moon?

I grabbed a flashlight from inside.

CHAPTER 69

❀ Ashley ❀

The girls' faces were lit orange by the fire. They were throwing marshmallows into the flames and watching them turn black.

"You should have seen that girl's leg," Denise said. "It was awful. I don't blame them for anything they do to that dog."

"Good thing you were there," Liz said.

I edged closer, trying to make them look at me, but the fire crackled and hissed. Finally, Liz looked up and screamed.

"It's just me," I said. I must have been scary looking, coming in from the darkness.

Denise put a hand over her chest. "I thought you were a bear. Mom saw one the other morning."

A man came to the door. “Everything all right?”

“It’s okay, Dad,” Denise said.

He studied me, took a sip of something, and moved back inside.

Liz pursed her lips and looked away, like I had a disease.

Finally, I put my hands out and warmed them by the fire. “Denise, can I ask you a question?”

She threw another marshmallow and it sizzled to death. When she had been alone earlier, she had seemed more open. Now, with Liz by her side, it was as if a door had closed.

“How did you know the girl was hurt?” I said.

“I heard her scream.”

“From where?”

“I told you. I was right here. She was yelling like she was dying.”

“And you ran to her?”

“After calling 911. But I guess she had already called, because the operator said she had just dispatched a squad car and an ambulance.”

“How long had you been out here?” I said.

Denise looked at me like it was none of my business, but she answered anyway. “I’d been sunbathing about a half hour.”

Liz sighed and crossed her arms. “I’m getting cold. Think I’ll go inside.”

“Did you actually see Buck bite her?”

“Did you see her leg? I didn’t have to actually see him chomping her.” She stood and followed Liz. When she reached the door she turned. “Face it, Timberline. That dog is a menace. I hope they’ve already gotten rid of it.”

CHAPTER 70

Bryce

I ran through the barn into the field, causing the alpacas to hum as I flew past. The black dot was gone now, so I figured it had just been my imagination.

The awful smell hit me again, like year-old dirty diapers mixed with rotten potato peels. I heard the heavy breathing again. Closer. Like Darth Vader breathing into a giant coffee can.

I pointed the flashlight toward the road. The breathing stopped, but that smell hung in the air. Two huge eyes glared back at me from the other side of the fence.

CHAPTER 71

✖ Ashley ✖

As I made my way back across the field I heard Bryce yell. A flashlight beam swung wildly behind the barn, then fell.

"Bear! Ashley, it's a bear!" he shouted.

I passed the barn and heard the alpacas humming. Bryce was throwing stones over the fence. I picked up the flashlight and pointed it toward the road. The bear was next to the fence. I pulled out Leigh's Mace, took a few steps toward the animal, and fired. I must have missed. On the third try the bear screamed—I didn't know they could—then ran away, swatting at its face with huge paws. The smell was awful. It was like Pippin and Frodo had spent a year inside our garbage.

Bryce turned, and I saw fear in his eyes. "We need to build a fire," he said. "Find kindling and I'll get wood."

We made two small piles, one near the barn and the other near where we'd seen the bear. We dug a trench around each pile so it wouldn't catch anything else on fire. Bryce lit the one by the barn, and I lit the one by the road. They were hard to start, but then they burned easily.

"Where were you, anyway?" Bryce said.

I told him what Denise had said. "Maybe the bear will take a dip in their pool."

"He could use some shampoo," Bryce said, crawling through the fence and moving through the ditch to the road. He was standing near where the girl had been attacked. He aimed the flashlight at the ground. At his feet was a hamburger wrapper from a fast-food restaurant. The burger was gone, but the bun lay on the ground, slathered with ketchup and mustard. "Litterbugs," he muttered.

"Think that's what the bear smelled?" I said.

Bryce shrugged. He picked up an empty plastic container, a little bigger than a nail polish bottle. It had a narrow, white tip. He pointed the flashlight at it. There were traces of red liquid inside. The label had been ripped off.

He stuffed it in his pocket, and we returned to the barn. "I ought to stay out here tonight," he said. "The fire will probably keep the bear away, but without Buck I want to be sure."

"I'm not staying inside by myself," I said.

He nodded. "Let's look for some sleeping bags."

CHAPTER 72

◉ *Bryce* ◉

I woke up to something sniffing my face. I thought it was the bear and almost yelled before I remembered where I was and realized it was an alpaca. I sat up on my soft bed of hay in the barn. The animals were up, and the sun was peeking through the boards.

Ashley and I smelled like the fires, which had burned out. At least we had kept the animals safe. Whitney was standing still, but when Ashley moved toward her, she jumped. I guess she'd been sleeping.

We gave the alpacas their food and water, then carried our sleeping bags to the house. I pulled out the tube I had stuck in my pocket the night before and held it under the light in the kitchen. It had turned upside down, and a red spot dotted my pocket. I squeezed a drop of the stuff onto my finger. It didn't smell like nail polish.

Ashley said, "Remember that play in sixth grade? I had to put fake blood on my arm. That's the kind of bottle the stuff came in. Bryce, what if the girl—?" She stopped and pointed to the answering machine, which was blinking.

I pushed the button.

"Ashley, this is Officer Tolson from the sheriff's department. Got your message this morning. We haven't been able to get in touch with the Morrises, so if you hear from them, please have them call. Animal control said they had to tranquilize the dog to get him out of the truck.

"Normally we'd keep an animal like this until we can make a determination. But I have to be honest. We heard from the girl's father yesterday, and he wants the animal destroyed. I'm sorry, but I guess we don't have a choice."

Ashley picked up the phone, shaking. "Bryce, Buck didn't do anything to that girl." She dialed, her lip trembling.

I took the phone from her, and she looked relieved.

The officer answered, sounding like he was in his car. I told him who I was. "Have they already . . . ?"

"Put him to sleep? Not yet."

"When?"

He paused. "Unless we hear from the owners, the vet will put him down first thing Monday morning at nine."

CHAPTER 73

✾ Ashley ✾

Officer Tolson's words haunted me as we drove our ATVs home that morning.

I was afraid Mom wouldn't let us stay at the Morrises' that night, and that was the only way we were going to protect the alpacas and catch the thieves.

We hurried inside for breakfast. Mom smiled. "Is Leigh going to be gone tonight?" I said as she broke some eggs into a bowl.

"She and Randy are going to a movie. She should be back late. Why?"

"Bryce and I want to stay at the farm again."

Bryce groaned as he opened the paper. "The Cubs traded one of their best pitchers to the Mets!"

"I don't know if that's a good idea," Mom said.

"It was a terrible idea," Bryce said.

"No, about staying there tonight. If Leigh isn't here and you need her—"

"Mom, I have to see that game. They've got this new TV—it's like being at Wrigley."

I'll admit ganging up on Mom was unfair. "You told Mrs. Henderson you like to say yes to us as often as you can," I said. "That if you can't think of a good reason to say no, you try to let us do what we want."

She rolled her eyes. "You both look like you didn't sleep well."

"It was a lot of fun," I said.

"Well, as long as that dog is there, I feel a lot better."

I sneaked a glance at Bryce, but he just stared at the newspaper. Not telling her everything was like lying. Normally I could tell her anything.

Mom finally gave in, on the condition that we take naps that afternoon. That made me feel like a little kid, but keeping stuff from her made me feel terrible. I tried to tell myself I had no choice and that it was the only way to protect the alpacas, save Buck, and catch the criminals.

CHAPTER 74

Bryce

Being in a cage must be the worst for a dog that is usually able to run in big fields. Everything in him must have wanted to go home and protect his herd.

Then again, maybe it was like vacation. Meals brought to your kennel. You could lounge around and talk with the other campers. As much as I tried to make it funny, Buck was on death row. If we didn't do something fast, his owners would return to find his grave.

Ashley and I went back to the farm before dinner and made sure the alpacas were okay. There were no more signs of the bear, but the animals stayed close to the barn. I guess they sensed Buck wasn't there and didn't want to take any chances.

We walked through the house trying to figure out what Eddie might be looking for. The big television was the only thing worth a lot of money. That and the leather couch, I guess.

"Has to be something else," Ashley said. "Who would risk trying to lug that out of here?"

We went through the bedrooms and found Mrs. Morris's jewelry box. There wasn't much inside, and I figured she just wasn't a jewelry person. Downstairs was a den with a big deer head on the wall and a locked gun cabinet with a glass door. I counted six guns. I wondered what the bear's head would look like on the wall.

Ashley said, "What's this?"

I shrugged. It looked like an end table with a Southwestern-style blanket over it, colored triangles woven into the intricate design.

She picked up the lamp and pulled the blanket away. Underneath was a gray safe with a huge metal handle and tumblers the size of my hand. I spun the knob and heard the *click-click-click.*

"Maybe this is what they're after," I said.

"Wonder how they would know about it," Ashley said, looking around. "There's no window down here. If we can get them inside and jam the door from the outside, we'll catch the crooks. Then the police will have to believe us about Buck."

CHAPTER 75

❀ Ashley ❀

Mom looked concerned when we came back to the house for dinner. She motioned me into the kitchen and asked me to sit down. She only does that when there's a good reason, so I started getting nervous. "Denise's mother called today," she said.

"Oh?" I said as innocently as I could.

"She said you crept up on Denise and Liz and scared them last night."

"I didn't mean to," I said.

Mom put up a hand. "She said they saw two fires at the Morrises' last night. She wanted to know if you knew how dangerous that was."

I nodded. "We wanted to watch the animals, so we stayed in the barn. We dug a trench around the fires—"

"Ashley, you know how edgy people are about fire during the summer. You can't set campfires that close to the woods."

"It won't happen again," I said.

Mom pursed her lips. "Denise's mom also told me what happened with Buck."

I felt a lump in my throat. I was sure she wasn't going to let us stay at the farm, and I had to keep that from happening. I took a deep breath and closed my eyes.

"I've tried to call Mr. Morris," she said. "Can't get through."

"They're going to put Buck to sleep if we don't do something, Mom."

"You should have told me."

"I thought you wouldn't let us stay out there, and if anything happened to the alpacas—"

"You should have told me anyway."

"I promised I wouldn't let anything happen to him," I said, tearing up.

"If you and Bryce want to stay the night again, it's okay. I just don't want you outside. Understand?"

I nodded.

"Pastor Andy called and wants to talk to you. I saw him at the grocery store yesterday and told him what you were doing this weekend. He wondered if you'd do a short devotional before Sunday school. He said you could tell what you've learned about alpacas."

"I'm not sure I've learned anything."

"Call him. Maybe by tomorrow something will come to mind."

CHAPTER 76

☺ *Bryce* ☺

I wondered why Pastor Andy didn't ask me to talk abut the alpacas, which is probably why I started calling my sister Reverend Ashley. Later I taped a sign on her door: "Saint Ashley of the Alpacas."

We thought about parking our ATVs in the barn to keep them out of sight, but Ashley was afraid that would scare Whitney. We drove them into the woods behind the house and hid them behind some brush. We didn't want the thieves to show up and see somebody in the house.

I found a two-by-four we could wedge under the door handle to the den. We tried it out with Ashley inside and me locking her in.

She pushed and pushed but couldn't get the door open. We also made a hiding place beneath the stairs where we could wait for the intruders. I would call 911 from the Morrises' cordless phone as soon as anyone entered the house.

Though the TV wasn't as good as the one upstairs, I watched the Cubs game in the den so no one could see it glowing from outside. They led the Cardinals until the ninth inning. Two outs, two on, two runs ahead, the pitcher gave up a home run and the Cubs were down a run. They almost scored in the bottom of the inning, but a guy got thrown out at home for the third out. I don't believe in luck, good or bad, but I'd say the Cubs have had their share of the bad.

We checked the alpacas one more time before we holed up for the night. Ashley said she thought Whitney didn't seem to be humming as much. I said she should take Whitney to church and see if she could teach her "Amazing Grace."

CHAPTER 77

✿ Ashley ✿

Bryce and I sat in the dark under the stairs, listening, the heavy blanket from the safe draped over the opening. We had pillows and a flashlight, the two-by-four, and Leigh's can of Mace. (She noticed it was missing, and I asked to borrow it one more night.)

It got creepily quiet, and every creak and noise made me think someone was there.

Bryce asked what I was going to talk about in Sunday school the next morning.

"Psalm 23," I said.

"I thought that was about sheep."

"Yeah, but any animal will do."

"What's the point of the . . . you know, the message?" He seemed interested, not just wanting to make fun of me.

I shrugged. "I guess I'll talk about how peaceful they are and how much they trust their owners. That they don't worry about anything when they're being taken care of."

I pulled out my notes. "I wrote down the verbs, all the stuff a shepherd does for his flock. 'Leads, renews, guides, prepares, honors, anoints.'" I had written several sentences for each, using characteristics of alpacas I had found on different Web sites.

"That's pretty good," Bryce said. I was waiting for some joke, but he said, "Don't you wish Dad could be here to read that?"

"I always wish Dad could be here. Except . . ."

"What?"

"I don't know. I wonder why God let him die. I don't think we'll ever figure it out, but I wonder if part of it has something to do with us becoming a family with Sam and Leigh."

"God would kill Dad for that?"

"No, I don't mean that. It's like the verse that says whatever happens to a Christian, God can make something good out of it, even if it's bad."

"And what if Sam and Leigh never believe in Jesus?"

"Guess we have to rest like the alpacas, believe God knows what he's doing, and have a little faith."

CHAPTER 78

Bryce

My back ached and my butt felt so numb I doubted I could ever stand. You could have hit me with the two-by-four and I never would have felt it. All I heard was the creaky house and the wind. I put my head back against the wall and closed my eyes.

When the Morrises' cordless rang, I nearly threw the thing through the wall. I looked at my watch—11:45.

The Morrises didn't have caller ID.

"Should we answer?" I said. "It could be Mr. Morris."

"It could be Eddie and his people."

"It could be Mom."

"Just pick it up and don't say anything," Ashley said.

"Hello?" Lewis said upstairs. "Hello? Thank you for calling!"

I mashed the Speakerphone button and heard something like a rushing wind. "Sam?" I said.

Click.

Ashley shook her head. "Why did you do that?"

I couldn't speak. Had I just given us away?

CHAPTER 79

Ashley

The phone rang again, and I felt like throwing up. Bryce looked at me, and we didn't have to say anything. We just let it ring. The answering machine picked up upstairs, and when the beep finally sounded, whoever it was hung up.

"What time is it?" I said.

Bryce hit the light on his watch. "Midnight. Couple minutes before."

Suddenly my heart leaped. *My medicine!*

I have to take medicine for a seizure disorder. If I don't, my brain gets messed up and I can pass out.

I pulled the capsules from my pocket. “I need water.”

“Bathroom’s down the hall.”

“I’m not going alone.”

I couldn’t see, but I’m sure Bryce rolled his eyes. “Come on,” he said.

We felt our way down the dark hallway and found the bathroom. I cupped my hand under the faucet, popped the pills into my mouth, and slurped until they went down.

After another half hour of seat-numbing sitting, we were antsy for the robbers. It was like waiting for Christmas, only you didn’t want it to come. I wanted to catch these thieves, but if any part of our plan went wrong . . .

Finally, Bryce said, “Let’s go upstairs and have a look.”

CHAPTER 80

Bryce

I could tell Ashley was scared by the way she stayed really close, but I was just as scared. What if Eddie had parked at the gate and walked to the house? What if he and whoever was helping him were already inside or watching through the windows?

We had left the range light on in the kitchen, so we stopped when we got near the top of the steps and looked around. Everything was quiet. Ashley pushed me, but I stayed where I was.

"Come on, Bryce!" she whispered.

Something moved outside—past the patio door. Animal or human, I couldn't tell, but something was out there. I motioned for Ashley to go back downstairs. We hurried, trying not to make noise on the steps.

Back in our hideout, I told Ashley what I had seen.

"They're out there?" she said.

"It could have been Mr. Bear, which might be worse. I say we stay here until we hear them come in the house."

"Wouldn't they have pulled the trailer close to put the stuff in?" Ashley said. "They're not going to lug that safe all the way to the road."

"Maybe they're making sure things are clear, and then they'll pull it up to the house."

"Either way, I think we should call the police. It'll take them a long time to get out here."

"The plan was to wait until they—"

"Plans change," she said, and I could hear the emotion in her voice. "It's better if they catch them pulling out with all the stuff than to not catch them at all. What time is it?"

I hit my watch light again. A half hour had passed, and it seemed like two weeks. "Okay, I'll call."

I hit the Talk button and started dialing. The beeps sounded, but when I held the phone up to my ear there was nothing. I clicked the Talk button off, then turned it on again and listened.

"No dial tone," I said. "I'll use my cell." I dug it out and punched it on. Nothing.

"Don't tell me you left it on!" she hissed.

"I thought I recharged it."

She grabbed it and punched the top button, frantically trying to turn it on. Then she took the other phone and tried again.

I tried to smile. "Maybe the bear cut the line."

"Not funny," she said. "What now?"

"Plan B."

CHAPTER 81

❀ Ashley ❀

I didn't care what Plan B was. I just wanted to do something.

Bryce totally caught me off guard. He burst out of our hiding place and turned on every light he could find. "You take upstairs!" he yelled.

I raced up, keeping a close watch on the patio door and the windows. I turned on all the lights in the bedrooms, and when I came out the radio and TV were blaring. The light coming from the house lit up the yard, and the noise was deafening.

"What are we doing?" I hollered.

He bolted into the kitchen and threw open the cabinets.

"Letting them know we're here. They'll leave when they see what's going on."

"But don't we want to catch them?"

"Not tonight," Bryce said. He pulled out two huge boiling pots and handed me a wooden spoon. "Pretend it's New Year's!"

We beat on those pots like we were in a rock band. I'm not proud of it, but I imagined Liz's face on my pot and whacked it even harder.

Bryce moved toward the window, something I wasn't ready to do. His eyes grew wide, and he dropped his pot and spoon and hurried to the front door.

"What?" I screamed, but he was already outside.

I followed him into the yard and toward the barn. Taillights flashed as a trailer bounced down the dusty road.

"Come on!" Bryce yelled.

My fear of the robbers left when I saw the barn door open and several alpacas out, humming loudly under the moonlit sky. Bryce flicked on the fluorescent lights inside. We counted the animals and came up five short.

"Count again," Bryce said.

"Wait," I said, running toward the back of the barn. "Where's Whitney?"

CHAPTER 82

☺ *Bryce* ☺

I kicked myself for not figuring it out. Eddie couldn't have known about the Morrises' safe anyway. He had gotten the trailer to steal alpacas.

"Go to Denise's and call the police," I said. "I'll try to follow them."

I knew Ashley didn't want to go back to Denise's place any more than I wanted to chase alpaca thieves on my own, but I wasn't about to let them get away without a fight. I ran to my ATV in the underbrush and tried to drive around the trees, but the fence blocked me. I circled back, found a small clearing through the woods, and shot out the other side.

The moon made driving over unfamiliar territory a little easier as I sped down the hill to the road. The taillights of the trailer glowed in the distance. The road was so bumpy that there was no way they could drive fast, so I thought I had a chance.

It reminded me of the old joke about a dog chasing a car—what would he do when he caught it? I didn't know, but I wasn't about to stop.

When I got to the road I pushed the thumb accelerator all the way and let the four-wheeler go as fast as it could. When the road curved I saw the truck and trailer pulling onto the main road to my left. They were only about a quarter of a mile ahead, so I shifted my weight and kept the accelerator down as I rounded the corner.

Something black darted across my path and I swerved to miss it, but the ATV plunged off the road.

CHAPTER 83

❀ Ashley ❀

I knocked lightly at Denise's, hoping somebody might be awake. When no one answered, I rang the doorbell.

I looked through the little windows beside the door and saw someone marching down the stairs in a long robe. I backed away as the light came on and the door unlocked. It was Denise's father, and he was clearly angry.

"Sorry to wake you, but my brother and I are watching the Morrises' farm and—"

"Haven't you caused enough trouble?"

"I just need to use your phone—"

"Your mother assured my wife you wouldn't bother us again, and look at the time!"

"But, Mr. Ruger—"

"Get out of here now! Understand?"

I ran to my ATV without looking back. I roared up the road to the next house and slid to the porch. These people had to be nicer than the Rugers.

An old man came to the door, adjusting his hearing aid.

"Please!" I said. "I need to use your phone. There's been a robbery."

His wife joined him, looking suspicious. "Where?"

When I told them, the woman took my arm. "You poor thing. Come on inside."

Her kindness nearly made me cry as I choked out the details. The man kept adjusting his hearing aid.

"Call the police," she told him.

A few moments later her husband brought me the phone. "They want to talk to you," he said.

I told them everything, even why we thought it was Eddie, but they said to save that for the officer who would arrive shortly.

I called Mom, and about half an hour later she showed up with Bryce, who had scratches all over him.

"What happened to you?"

"Had a run-in with a bear . . . or something that crossed the road just as I was about to catch those guys. Plowed into some scrub oak."

We thanked the old couple profusely, and I followed Mom and Bryce to the farm in time to meet the officer. He said they had found the phone wires cut at the back of the Morris house. He wrote down everything we told him, including what Bryce had learned at Carhardt's Garage.

The officer pushed his hat back and studied us. "How do you know all that about this Eddie character?"

Bryce hesitated, looking at me, Mom, then the officer. "I overheard him talking about it."

"When?"

He looked at Mom again.

She sighed. "It's okay. I know you were at the garage."

Bryce looked as stunned as I felt. How in the world . . . ?

Bryce told the officer everything. The officer snapped his writing pad shut and put it in his pocket.

"What about Buck?" I said.

The officer turned. "Who's Buck?"

When I told him he said, "I don't see how this changes anything. A dog that attacks like that has to be dealt with."

"But if it's all a plot—I mean, if we could prove Buck didn't really bite the girl, wouldn't that change things?"

The officer nodded. "Sure."

CHAPTER 84

Bryce

Mom told us to go to bed and that she would tell Pastor Andy we wouldn't be at church for Ashley's devotion. I dreamed we were crying at the edge of a grave as Buck's casket was lowered by two alpacas. Three others held guns on their shoulders and fired into the air seven times. An alpaca 21-gun salute. Mr. Morris and his family wouldn't even look at Ashley and me.

When I awoke and went downstairs, I found Ashley with Mom, who was on the phone with someone at the sheriff's office, pleading for Buck's life.

When Mom hung up she said, "There's nothing they can do, no one they can talk to until tomorrow morning."

"But that's when they're going to kill Buck!" Ashley said.

"We have to find the jogger," I said.

"But the police and the paramedic won't give us the name," Ashley said.

"Someone else knows who she is."

"Right," Ashley said. "Eddie."

"Someone else."

"Who?"

"The only other person who saw her. Denise."

CHAPTER 85

❀ Ashley ❀

Bryce walked, and I drove my ATV to where he had crashed the night before. Bryce's vehicle was buried in the scrub oak and scratched up, but we were able to get it out and head to the farm. We had lost five alpacas worth tens of thousands of dollars. I prayed we'd get them back before the Morrises got home, but my biggest concern was Whitney. She was in no condition for a bumpy ride like that.

Every one of the others seemed spooked. Last night had taken its toll. After we fed them and while we were cleaning the stalls, a car pulled up to the front gate. Doors slammed.

I looked at Bryce. "Who could that be?"

We walked out to find three people heading toward us. Denise, her mom, and her dad.

"Get ready to get chewed out," I said.

Denise's dad spoke first. "Ashley?" He put his hand on Denise's shoulder and puffed his cheeks. "I want to apologize for last night. We heard what happened. I'm sorry I didn't listen to you."

I bit my lip and nodded.

"Denise told us what really happened at school and at the amusement park," her mom said. "We were unfair to you."

Denise looked at the ground and spoke softly. "I really didn't see that girl get attacked." I wondered if her parents made her say it.

"There may still be time to save Buck. Can you help us find the girl?"

CHAPTER 86

Bryce

It was Ashley's idea to look at Leigh's high school yearbooks. She had two of them, so we started with the most recent.

Denise described the jogger as about Mom's height, long hair that looked dyed black, brown eyes, and a small mouth.

"Anything weird about her?" I said. "Scars or something?"

"Her hands were mostly red from the blood," Denise said. "But she had dirty fingernails. And there was something on her arm, maybe a tattoo. Her sleeve covered most of it, but I think it was round."

"Her hair could be any color," Ashley said as she flipped through the yearbook. Denise picked out several girls who looked something like the jogger, and Ashley kept a list.

Sam's truck pulled up, and he ambled toward the house wearing sunglasses. His smile made deep lines in his face, and he hadn't shaved. "What's going on, Bryce?" he growled.

I followed him inside, telling him everything we knew about the case. He felt sure the police would find the alpacas. "The whole herd's been tagged electronically. You sure about this Eddie guy?"

"As sure as I can be," I said. "But he's not working alone. No way he could have taken those animals by himself."

"And this girl—"

"Bryce!" Ashley yelled.

I ran outside. Ashley had two yearbooks open. She pointed at a senior picture in one. "Denise thinks this might be her." She held up the other yearbook. It showed two girls in a hallway mugging for the camera, their sleeves rolled up and striking a muscle-man pose.

Denise said, "She has a tattoo on her arm."

The girl's hair was lighter than in the other picture, but the tattoo was there, and her face looked similar.

I read the name underneath the senior picture aloud. "Janice Snodgrass."

CHAPTER 87

❀ Ashley ❀

Things were coming together, and none too soon. Denise had to go home, and Bryce and I tore through the phone book looking for Snodgrass. There was only one listing.

An older woman answered. "Janice is my daughter," she said carefully. "Who is this?"

I told her my name. "She was attacked by our friend's dog, and my brother and I wanted to see how she was doing."

"You must have the wrong person," she said. "Janice hasn't been attacked by any dog."

"Can we talk with her?"

"I'll tell her you called."

We had to find Janice or Eddie if we wanted to save Buck.

"Let's pay a visit to Mrs. Snodgrass," Bryce said.

CHAPTER 88

Bryce

It was late in the afternoon when we parked our ATVs at Mrs. Watson's house and made our way through town. Mrs. Snodgrass's house sat across the street from an old elementary school near a dead oak tree. Her concrete porch was cracked and had pulled away from the house. The place looked big enough for one person, maybe two.

I knocked on the screen door, and it rattled against the frame. A white-haired woman with thin arms hobbled toward me. "Whatever it is, I don't want any."

"Not selling anything, ma'am. Just need to talk with Janice."

"She's not here."

"Know where I can find her?"

"She went camping with her boyfriend in the mountains."

"Sounds like fun," I said. "Do you know where?"

She shook her head. "They left yesterday afternoon pulling a big trailer—don't know what that was for. What do you need with her?"

"It's actually a matter of life and death," I said. I handed her a card with my cell phone number on it.

She looked at it skeptically and stuffed it into her apron.

We headed back to our ATVs. While Ashley stopped to see Mrs. Watson, I went to the court at the middle school where Toby was shooting hoops. I told him what had been going on and said, "Keep an eye out for a long trailer with alpacas in it."

CHAPTER 89

❀ Ashley ❀

I couldn't help imagining trying to explain what had happened to Buck and the Morrises trying to tell their boys why they didn't have a dog anymore. The whole thing felt hopeless. Buck was going to die. No question about it.

I was worried about Whitney too. I dug out the emergency number for the vet and was surprised when a woman answered. She knew Whitney well.

"You're right to be worried about her," she said. "Any kind of trauma could send her into labor, especially since she's this far along. They usually have their young before noon, and by evening the little things are up and running around. As soon as you find her, call me. I'll want to check her out."

CHAPTER 90

☺ *Bryce* ☺

It's hard trying to sleep when you know someone's going to die. Buck was just a dog, but he felt like a friend. I tossed and turned the whole night, looking at the clock.

At five Monday morning I went downstairs for breakfast. Ashley came down a few minutes after I did. Then Sam joined us. That was nice. He could have slept the whole day because of his late flight, and we wouldn't have blamed him.

"Mind if I come along to the farm and see you guys in action?" he said.

He drove us there and we checked the alpacas. Sam went to look at the house—cut phone cord and all—while we got the animals' water and food.

"What time is it?" Ashley said, as if she didn't really want to know.

"Almost seven."

"Two more hours," she said. "You suppose they give a dog a last meal like they do real criminals?"

I shrugged. "Maybe they let them chase a cat or something." I was trying to be funny, but neither of us laughed.

Sam helped us clear the alpaca poop, which was the most disgusting part of the job, and we got back in his truck.

My cell phone rang.

"Bryce, it's Toby. My dad thinks he knows where those alpacas are."

CHAPTER 91

❀ Ashley ❀

Sam drove while Bryce gave directions. Mr. Krenshaw had noticed something funny in a remote section off Dead Man's Pass, a winding road up the side of Memorial Mountain. An old hunting cabin that belonged to a friend of his sat on the road where he delivered papers. Normally a chain hooked to two timbers blocked anyone from coming onto the property, but the chain had been cut and deep tire marks marred the road.

Mr. Krenshaw had seen a long trailer parked in front of the cabin and called Toby on his CB radio before continuing his route.

As Bryce explained what had happened, Sam sped up. We made

it to Dead Man's Pass, turned left, and went straight up the mountain. It felt like we were entering another world.

"Why do they call this Dead Man's Pass?" I said.

"Wagon trains used to come through here," Sam said. "A few got snowed in and never made it out. Some of the old wagon parts are in a museum."

The road went from blacktop to gravel to dirt. I imagined Whitney riding over this and wondered if she had given birth.

When Bryce hung up with Toby, he dialed the sheriff's office and brought them up to speed.

"Should be around one more curve," Sam said.

I held my breath as the sun cast shadows through the pine trees, giving the whole area an eerie look.

"There!" Bryce said.

Sam pulled over and we got out. The chain had definitely been cut, and I saw the tracks in the dirt road.

We heard voices. Someone yelling. Glass crashing.

And the hum of alpacas.

CHAPTER 92

Bryce

Sam put a finger to his lips as we walked up the hill. I saw movement in the trailer, which had been unhitched from the truck. The alpacas fidgeted and hummed inside—they probably hadn't eaten for a whole day. When we moved around back we saw the truck parked among some bushes.

"You jerk, Eddie!" a female screamed inside the cabin. "You said you had this all worked out!"

"I did," Eddie said, "but things happen. I coulda let the guy take 'em yesterday, but not without the money. I'm not trustin' anybody to owe me that much."

"I can't stay here!" the girl shouted.

We hunkered low as we passed a window. I sneaked a peek inside and saw black hair on the girl's shoulder.

"Come on, honey. Calm down. If we can't sell them, you know the owners will offer a reward. Either way we're out of here."

"And how are we going to convince them we didn't steal them?"

"Trust me, Jan. They'll be so glad to get 'em back, there'll be no questions asked."

"I have trusted you, and look where it got me. I just want to go home."

Sam motioned us close and whispered, "Stay here. I'll head to the road and flag down the sheriff." He pulled a multi-tool gadget from his pocket. "If you get a chance and know you can do this without being seen or heard, pop the hood on that truck and unhook one of the battery cables."

Sam slipped into the brush like an animal stalking prey and was gone.

Ashley gasped. "Bryce, there's something wrong with Whitney."

Whitney was at the back of the trailer, away from the others, and they seemed to be nervously staying as far from her as possible too. When Whitney turned I saw blood on her hind legs.

"Give me your phone," Ashley whispered.

Just as I handed it to her, it rang. I hit the Off button as fast as I could, but Eddie and Janice stopped talking. "Did you hear that?" he said.

CHAPTER 93

❀ Ashley ❀

I said a bad word I'd have to get forgiveness for later, and I could only hope the two inside didn't hear that too.

"What?" Janice said.

"I heard a phone."

"You're imagining—"

"Shut up! I heard a phone!"

"Then somebody's found us!" she said.

"Whoever it is," Eddie said, "they have no idea who we are. Stay here."

"Eddie!" Janice whined.

"I'm just gonna look around. I'll be right back."

The back door opened and slammed. Then the truck engine revved. Tires spun and Eddie tore off down the hill. We heard the front door and slipped to the other side of the trailer, spooking the alpacas even more.

"Eddie!" Janice yelled, running out and down the driveway. She fell to her knees and cried, gushing swearwords as she balled her hands into fists and screamed.

"I know her!" Bryce whispered. "That's Jan from Instant Oil!"

I heard another engine and wondered if Sam was chasing Eddie. Why hadn't Bryce sabotaged that battery when he had the chance?

I jumped up and tore open the back door of the trailer. The other four alpacas gingerly stepped past Whitney and bounded out, probably starving.

"Give me the phone, Bryce!"

I didn't have the vet's number, so I called information and was connected in seconds. My hands shook as I crept closer to Whitney. "It's okay, girl. We're going to get you help."

When the vet answered I whispered desperately, "This is Ashley Timberline, and we found the alpacas."

"Okay, good." She sounded groggy. "Late night last night with a foal in Castle Rock."

"Sorry, but this is an emergency. Whitney's really agitated, and there's blood on her hind legs."

"Okay, look closely at her rear end and tell me what else you see."

While Bryce kept an eye on Janice, I tried to get behind Whitney, but she kept bumping against the trailer. "It's all right, girl," I said. "Just trying to help you." But suddenly she spat at me, thick, gooey liquid splashing my hair. I yelped, fearing that would have to get Janice's attention.

"What do you see, Ashley?"

Whitney turned for a second. "Oh no!" I said. "There's something black sticking out of her!"

"Ashley, listen. Do you see any hair on what's coming out of her?"

I ducked as Janice stomped back into the cabin and slammed the door. I don't think she saw us.

I looked as close as I could, wary of another spit. "No! Just black!"

"Those are the cria's feet, Ashley. And that's a problem. You're going to have to help her. Is there anyone with you?"

"My brother."

"Give him the phone. You're going to need both hands."

CHAPTER 94

Bryce

"You have to help your sister," the vet said. "Tell her exactly what I tell you, understand?"

I was glad I just had phone duty. I wouldn't have wanted Ashley's job.

"Grab the two legs sticking out and pull," I said, repeating everything the vet said.

"I don't think I can do this!"

"You have to, or the baby will die," I said. "Its head usually comes first. When you pull the legs out, it'll release the head and the baby will follow."

"There's not enough to grab onto yet!"

"When Whitney starts to push again, grab and pull."

"How will I know she's pushing?"

"The baby will slide forward a little and give you something more to grab—"

"She's pushing!"

"Good! Grab and pull."

I heard the front door and turned in time to see Janice, a cell phone to her ear, easing outside and staring at the four alpacas grazing nearby. When she noticed the trailer door was open, she squinted at me and her jaw dropped. "It's just a couple of kids," she said. "You'd better get your tail back here and get me, or—"

Ashley grunted and I turned back to see the legs of the baby alpaca straighten.

"What's happening, Bryce?" the vet said.

"The legs are out now—"

But before I could say anything more, Whitney pushed again and first the head, then the whole body slid out and plopped on the trailer floor.

"I did it!" Ashley said, laughing through tears.

Janice stepped off the porch and peeked in. "Eddie, one of these things just gave birth. Gross! Now we're probably in bigger trouble! Get back here or—"

"Tell Ashley good job," the vet said. "Whitney will ignore the baby for a while, so just make sure it's warm. Put some straw near it. And tell me how to get there."

CHAPTER 95

❋ Ashley ❋

I had seen our cat, Patches, have kittens, but I'd never seen anything like this. And of course I hadn't had to help Patches.

Janice moved away from the trailer and slapped her phone shut. "Hang up on me, you—"

Bryce found some straw in the trailer and tucked it around the baby, watching out for Whitney.

I wiped my hands on the grass and followed Janice to the steps of the cabin where she sat, her face red.

"Eddie left, huh?"

She shook her head and swore. "The bum. And to think I was going to marry him."

Bryce joined us. "Where'd you get that?" he said, pointing to her necklace.

Janice rolled her eyes. "He said it was just the start." She dug in her pocket and pulled out a handful of jewelry, including a gold wedding band.

"We know who some of that belongs to," I said. "That ring is Mrs. Watson's, the old lady—"

"I know. Here. Take it. I don't want it anymore."

"Didn't you feel bad taking all that stuff?" Bryce said.

"I didn't steal anything. I just helped with the keys."

"How?" I said.

She stared at me, as if wondering what the difference was now. "It's easy. I made imprints of house keys on a piece of putty. Then I'd make a new one on my dad's old key machine. He was a locksmith, and when he died we sold everything but that machine. I wish we'd sold that thing too."

A car roared up the road and Janice stood, as if looking for the best place to run.

"Wait," Bryce said. "You've got nowhere to go. Rat out Eddie and see if they'll go easy on you."

She sat back down, crying. "You're kinda smart for a little brat. Guess I don't owe him a thing."

"That dog never attacked you, did he?" I said.

She shook her head. "That was Eddie's idea. He would've done it except he's really scared of dogs. He had me take a hamburger out there and get the dog to come close so I could spray fake blood on its mouth. I sprayed the rest on my leg."

"They're going to put that dog to sleep because of you," I said. "What time is it, Bryce?"

"Eight thirty."

The shelter was at least a half hour away. "Will you tell them the truth, Janice? We might still be able to save Buck."

"They won't believe me."

I grabbed her arm, tears coming. "Do the right thing. Bryce and I will tell them you gave us this stuff back."

"There's more inside," she said.

"So will you do it? Please?"

CHAPTER 96

Bryce

The sheriff walked up the driveway with Sam close behind. Janice held her hands out as if offering to be cuffed. "That won't be necessary, ma'am," the sheriff said. "I can't transport a female without a matron here anyway."

"We have to stop Buck's execution!" Ashley said. "Janice will tell you he didn't really attack her. It was all a fake."

"It's true," Janice said. "Eddie put me up to it. That dog shouldn't die."

"Maybe your boyfriend got what was coming to him then," the cop said.

"He's not my boyfriend anymore," she said. "You catch him?"

"I followed him all the way down Dead Man's Pass," Sam said. "When he saw me he lost control. Turned over in a field."

"Is he okay?" Janice said.

"He's shook up," the sheriff said. "A few scratches. Nothing compared to what's waiting for him in prison."

"What about Buck?" Ashley said. "We have to do something now!"

"I'll handle that," the sheriff said. He turned toward the radio strapped to his shoulder and called in, asking for a matron and also that a cruiser be dispatched to animal control to stop the procedure on Buck.

"Can't we just call them, sir?" the voice came back.

"If they were answering the phone, son, I wouldn't be requesting a cruiser, would I?"

"Thing is, sir, we don't have a car within an hour of there."

"We've got just enough time if you go now!" Ashley said. "Please!"

"I can't leave this prisoner," the sheriff said, "and I can't stay here with her alone either."

"We have to do *something*!" Ashley said.

The cop sighed. "Why don't you stay with us and let your dad and brother go to animal control?"

"I want to go," Ashley said.

"You can't have it both ways, little lady."

I knew Ashley hated it when people called her names like that.

Just then the vet's car came sliding up, our answer to everything. As she jogged to the trailer Ashley got her to agree to stay with the sheriff and his prisoner until the matron got there and even to help round up the other alpacas.

The sheriff handed Sam his card and said, "Give them this and tell them I said to hold off until I can get there. Go!"

Ashley and I ran to the truck, and Sam shot down Dead Man's Pass as fast as any human had ever dared.

I punched Redial for animal control, just in case, but the recording came on again.

"How long will it take us?" Ashley said as Sam skidded onto the I-25 ramp.

"Depends on traffic. Twenty, maybe 25 minutes."

"It's 8:46," I said, a tremble in my voice.

CHAPTER 97

✽ Ashley ✽

I felt the seconds rush by like a stream over rocks. In *The Wizard of Oz* Dorothy watched the sand slip through the hourglass, waiting for the witch to end her life. I always wanted Dorothy to turn the glass over and fool the witch. But there was no way to fool the clock now.

"If only we'd found those alpacas sooner," I said.

"You're lucky you found them at all," Sam said.

"No, this was not luck," I said, really trying to believe it. "I think it was God."

"Please, God," Bryce whispered, "don't let them do anything to Buck."

We passed exit after exit, until finally we saw the Air Force Academy on our right. The chapel, with its tall spires. The football field with *Air Force* printed on the stands. Parachutes opened to our right. I usually watch in awe as jumpers float to the ground, but now I focused on the road.

Bryce looked at me. "8:59," he said.

"Can't we go faster?" I said.

Sam hit the brakes as we ran up on cars slowing in the left lane. "Going as fast as I can."

I imagined a long needle in Buck's neck.

CHAPTER 98

Bryce

I dialed the animal shelter as soon as my watch clicked 9:00 and slammed my fist against the dashboard when I got the recording again.

"Hang on," Sam said as he careened off the interstate.

"Please, God," Ashley whispered.

"There it is!" I yelled, pointing to the sign above the building. Sam drove onto the sidewalk, through a patch of grass, over a concrete curb that circled the parking lot, and slid to a stop.

Ashley and I leaped out and hit the front door, racing inside. The clock said 9:06.

Two people stood waiting at the front desk—a man holding a small dog and a woman with an ancient poodle on a leash.

No one was behind the counter.

Ashley hit a small bell several times. When a woman came around the corner Ashley said, "We're here about the big white dog—you have to stop them."

The poodle made a puddle.

"You'll need to wait your turn," the woman said, then turned to the man with the dog.

"Please," Ashley said. "They're going to put a dog down, but he didn't do anything."

"It's all right," the man said. "You can go ahead."

But the worker behind the counter just glared at us.

"A white dog was brought in for attacking someone, but he didn't do it and we have proof. The sheriff—"

"They've already started on that dog," the woman said.

"No!" Ashley screamed.

"If you don't calm down—"

"What room are they in?" Sam's voice boomed behind us.

"Operating room one," she said. "But—"

I ran past the counter and burst through a door marked Employees Only that led to a hall with closed doors on both sides.

The woman from the desk was right behind me as I flew down the hall, looking for room one.

"Buck!" I shouted. "Buck, we're here!" I prayed I'd hear him bark.

At the end of the hall I found room one and threw the door open. A man wearing a light blue smock and holding a long needle looked up. Buck lay still on a metal table, eyes closed.

"No," I breathed. "Buck, no!"

The woman grabbed my arm and pulled me back, but I wrenched free as Ashley and Sam caught up.

"The sheriff sent us," I said. "Have you already—?"

"No, I just gave him a relaxant to make it easier for him. He's been so friendly and gentle."

"He's not dead?" I said.

"Just sleeping," the man said. "He won't feel a thing." He gestured with the syringe. "This is the lethal dose. You got here just in time. If I hadn't stopped at Tasty Kreme, I'd be done already."

Sam showed the vet the sheriff's card and explained what he had said. He set the syringe aside and wheeled Buck into a large cage. "He'll sleep a long time," he said. "But he'll be fine."

Ashley went and stroked Buck's fur. "It's okay now, boy. You're going home soon."

CHAPTER 99

❀ Ashley ❀

We drove straight from the shelter to Mrs. Watson's house. Peanuts barked when Bryce knocked, and it took Mrs. Watson quite a while to get there. She seemed tired.

"Well, why is everybody smiling?" she said. "Looks like a party."

"It is," Bryce said. "Lots to celebrate."

He showed her the brooch, coins, and other jewelry that had been stolen. "Recognize them?"

Mrs. Watson's mouth fell open as she examined the valuables. "Where in the world . . . ?"

I told her in one long run-on sentence, but I could tell she got lost somewhere between Buck getting taken away and finding Janice at the cabin.

"Little Jan," she said. "So sweet. Who'd have guessed?"

Bryce dug in his pocket. "There's one more."

Mrs. Watson held the wedding ring like it was worth a million dollars, even though it was probably the least expensive piece that had been stolen. It dazzled in the morning light.

A tear leaked down her wrinkled face, and life seemed to spring into her eyes. She clutched the ring to her chest, her lip quivering. "How can I ever thank you?"

Bryce and I didn't need any more reward than the look on her face.

CHAPTER 100

Bryce

Mom said she could never have made up a story that suspenseful.

"You think God made the animal-control guy stop at the donut place?" Ashley said.

"Oh, please," Leigh said, sitting at the table eating breakfast.

"Whether it was God or just his stomach," Mom said, "the point is Buck is safe."

We learned later that Eddie was charged with burglary and that most of the stolen items were found in the cabin. The sheriff told Sam that Janice was cooperating and that he'd see what they could do for her.

We met the vet at the Morris farm that evening. She had gotten the other alpacas in the trailer and driven them home. The baby was already up and walking, and Whitney looked protective but much calmer.

"These animals owe their lives to you two," the vet said. "They were close to dehydrated. It wouldn't have been long."

Ashley gave her devotion at the youth group that Wednesday night. Everybody liked the baby alpaca story best.

We saw Liz and Denise in town the next day at the Toot Toot Café, but they pretended not to see us.

Ashley shrugged. "I would have expected more from Denise, but when she gets around Liz . . ."

"You still quitting band?" I said.

"Nope," Ashley said. "I've decided I'm not going to let them determine what I do and don't do. I may even practice over the summer."

CHAPTER 101

❀ Ashley ❀

Two days later the Morris family was home and Buck was back in the field, running and barking. The alpacas were doing well, especially Whitney.

Mr. Morris led us into the field where the new baby was running and nipping at grass. She was mostly white with a little black spot on the back of her head.

"What are you going to call her?" Bryce asked.

"Usually we try to come up with something that happened at the time of the cria's birth to help us name it. Snowbank was born during a huge storm last year. Straight A came the day we gave our oldest son his first report card. So, we thought we'd call this one . . ." He looked at us with eyebrows raised.

"What?" I said.

"We were thinking Rescue, but I suppose you two can name her whatever you like."

"Us?" I said.

"Yeah. My wife and I were going to give you and Bryce $20 a day each, but the more we talked about it, the more we realized Rescue wouldn't even be here if it wasn't for you. So, instead of paying you, we'd like to give her to you."

I couldn't breathe. Our own alpaca!

Rescue toddled up to Bryce and sniffed his shoe. I put out my hand, and she let me pet her. Whitney walked up humming. It almost sounded like "Amazing Grace."

And that's what we changed her name to.

About the Authors

Jerry B. Jenkins (jerryjenkins.com) is the writer of the Left Behind series. He owns the Jerry B. Jenkins Christian Writers Guild, an organization dedicated to mentoring aspiring authors. Former vice president for publishing for the Moody Bible Institute of Chicago, he also served many years as editor of *Moody* magazine and is now Moody's writer-at-large.

His writing has appeared in publications as varied as *Reader's Digest, Parade, Guideposts,* in-flight magazines, and dozens of other periodicals. Jenkins's biographies include books with Billy Graham, Hank Aaron, Bill Gaither, Luis Palau, Walter Payton, Orel Hershiser, and Nolan Ryan, among many others. His books appear regularly on the *New York Times, USA Today, Wall Street Journal,* and *Publishers Weekly* best-seller lists.

Jerry is also the writer of the nationally syndicated sports story comic strip *Gil Thorp,* distributed to newspapers across the United States by Tribune Media Services.

Jerry and his wife, Dianna, live in Colorado and have three grown sons and three grandchildren.

Chris Fabry is a writer and broadcaster who lives in Colorado. He has written more than 40 books, including collaboration on the Left Behind: The Kids series.

You may have heard his voice on Focus on the Family, Moody Broadcasting, or Love Worth Finding. He has also written for Adventures in Odyssey and Radio Theatre.

Chris is a graduate of the W. Page Pitt School of Journalism at Marshall University in Huntington, West Virginia. He and his wife, Andrea, have been married 22 years and have nine children, two birds, two dogs, and one cat.

RED ROCK MYSTERIES

#1 Haunted Waters

#2 Stolen Secrets

#3 Missing Pieces

#4 Wild Rescue

#5 Grave Shadows

#6 Phantom Writer

#7 Double Fault

#8 Canyon Echoes

#9 Instant Menace

#10 Escaping Darkness

#11 Windy City Danger

#12 Hollywood Holdup

#13 Hidden Riches

#14 Wind Chill

#15 Dead End

BRYCE AND ASHLEY TIMBERLINE are normal 13-year-old twins, except for one thing—they discover action-packed mystery wherever they go. Wanting to get to the bottom of any mystery, these twins find themselves on a nonstop search for truth.

CP0140